Second Hand Scott

G. A. Milnthorpe

PNEUMA SPRINGS PUBLISHING UK

First Published in 2017 by:
Pneuma Springs Publishing

Second Hand Scott
Copyright © 2017   G. A. Milnthorpe
ISBN13: 9781782284390

Gavin Milnthorpe has asserted his right under the Copyright, Designs and
Patents Act, 1988, to be identified as Author of this Work

British Library Cataloguing in Publication Data. A catalogue record for
this book is available from the British Library.

Pneuma Springs Publishing
A Subsidiary of Pneuma Springs Ltd.
7 Groveherst Road, Dartford Kent, DA1 5JD.
E: admin@pneumasprings.co.uk
W: www.pneumasprings.co.uk

For Beck, Charlie & Poppy.

And for all those who have ever felt second hand

1 Peter 5 v.10

Chapter 1

"Boring"

Project #13 - Bernice the Boring (very unsuccessful)

"You smile too much."

Bernice was sitting in front of me, a grumpy look on her grumpy face.

"You make it sound like a bad thing…" I said, with a smile on my face.

"It is."

Bernice pulled her orange cardigan tight around her substantial body and folded her arms under her humungous breast bastions; her habitual defensive posture.

"I used to find it endearing but now I just find it annoying." Bernice's northern drawl was loud. Loud, loud.

"I am sorry. I could try to smile less." (Still smiling).

"No, that won't do any good. It's not just the smiling, it's you really. I used to find you endearing, but now I just find you annoying."

"Oh."

This was a new kind of break up for me. Most of the girls I had ever broken up with (or who had broken up with me…to be more accurate) had been quite apologetic. They usually felt guilty. They wrung their hands and sat uncomfortably. They would cry or at least pretend to. They indulged in meaningless friendly small talk to create the flimsy pretence that we were, and always would be, friends…before eventually getting round to the business at hand – dumping me.

But Bernice – "I call a spade a spade" – Nicholls was different. She enjoyed being rude under the pretence of "honesty." She revelled in the phrase, "I am just being true to myself," as a means of contriving insulting situations, often with the more attractive girls at work.

She had been one of my least successful Projects.

She had a pretty face really, when it wasn't scowling. She had a timeless quality to her; in that you could tell she was young but you could also see exactly what she would look like as an old lady. Replace her gleaming white teeth with a set of falsies, put a few streaks of grey in her hair, and voila.

She was a rather thick set girl. (I could never decide if that was due to big bones or a really thick skin). But her size didn't make her cuddly or jolly (like Santa), but rather robust and unapproachable. Like a fortress.

"It's hard to be with someone who is relentlessly chirpy. It's draining. You never say a bad word about anyone. You're never negative about anything."

"And that's a bad thing is it?"

Bernice sighed, "No, but it's very boring."

Boring.

I have often found that Fate or God or just good old fashioned Sod's Law has a way of kicking me in the teeth with a flamboyant and ironic circumstantial flourish.

Boring.

That was the very reason Bernice had found herself recently single enough to attract my attention just a few months before.

She was having a cigarette in the designated smoking area outside my workplace. I could see her from my window. I would often stand by the window (to avoid doing work) and watch these desperately addicted people inhale small quantities of harmful chemicals in to their bodies, before heading back to work refreshed and becalmed – only to return two hours later for a further fix.

Bernice tended to frequent the smoking area three or four times a day. I enjoyed watching Bernice because you could tell her mood from about a hundred metres away. Her body language would radiate (negative) emotions. The way she walked conveyed her (bad) humour. It was generally grumpiness but occasionally, for a change, it would be rage. (Very, very occasionally, she looked borderline happy and she would engage her fellow smokers in pleasant chat. But those days were few and far between and her fellow smokers were always wary of this change of demeanour – like it was the trick of some cunning predator).

On that particular day, she had stomped to the smoking area, a thundercloud in her face. The smoking area cleared out pretty quickly as she set herself to violent inhalation. When she smoked her third consecutive cigarette I sensed that something significant might be amiss. The defiant set of her jaw and the bewildered occasional shakes of her head told me it was Man Trouble. Just my kind of thing. I went down to speak to her.

"He said I was boring."

I had to take up smoking (menthol) to win her trust and I had to spend weeks "accidentally" bumping into her at the smoking area.

Whilst the other Cancer Flirts tried to ignore Bernice, I actively lured her into conversation. We spoke about the weather (which annoyed her) and the delays on the trains (which infuriated her) and then about her job (which was horrendous) and her workmates (who were cretins). I smiled and commiserated and probed for the juicy stuff – her love life - and eventually she opened up about the man who had broken her heart – David, a Pensions' Officer from the local council.

"I mean, how can a Pensions' Officer call me boring? As if." She snorted (like a bull) to convey her contempt for that notion. "He said I never wanted to do anything. He said I never wanted to go anywhere. He said I never wanted to meet anyone. He said I was the most boring person he had ever met. As if."

I repeated the words "As if" as loudly as I could to signal my agreement. I added a snort (pig-like rather than bullish) for good measure. Bernice seemed to appreciate my affirmation. She glanced at me up and down, taking in my slim form, my strong arms and my happy, gormless, slightly chubby face. She offered me a cigarette, which I took. And Project number 13 (unlucky for some) was underway.

Over the course of the next four months I soon found out that "As if" was her favourite phrase.

"Shall we go...?"

"Shall we watch...?"

"Shall we have...?"

As if.

So, taking the hint, I stopped asking and we settled into a quiet life of staying in (at her house, not mine) or visiting her mother.

If we were at Bernice's house we would spend the majority of our time in her garden. Greenery was the only thing in the world that she appeared to rather like. I would be compelled to get down and dirty with her which, unfortunately, isn't a euphemism.

If we were at Bernice's mother's house we would spend all our time sitting around the kitchen table smoking cigarettes and drinking tea. They would talk and I would listen. It was tremendously boring but I smiled and made the most of it in the hope that Bernice might see something noble and inspirational in my non-participatory attitude to gossip. (She didn't).

And then...

"You never ask me to go out anymore."

I usually see a progression in my Projects. First they are upset (at being dumped), then they are angry (about being dumped), then they feel insecure (because they were dumped), then they are resolute to start again (despite the dumping).

They then become optimistic and interested in life again. They take up hobbies and buy new things. They invest in a new wardrobe (clothing not furniture). They meet new people or see old people in a new light. They start to look around them and see happiness lurking around the corner, a promised land that these broken creatures never thought they'd see again. Then they see me – encouraging, complimentary, accepting, smiling me – and they realise that the happiness around the corner does not involve me. The Promised Land is not for the likes of me. I'm "too nice." I'm "like a brother." I'm a "really good friend." They then become slightly ashamed as they dump me.

But not Bernice. She was grumpy at the start and grumpy at the end. Mercifully, there wasn't too much time in between. My attempts to lighten her outlook on life had failed miserably. She could even have been grumpier at the end than she was at the beginning.

"I think I'm supposed to say "Scott, it's not you, it's me.""

Bernice had invited me to meet her in a coffee shop in town. I knew something was amiss because this was an uncharacteristic move on her part. Bernice didn't like going out unless accompanied by her mother. She wasn't overly keen on spending money, except on cigarettes and begonias. And she certainly didn't like going for a coffee which she deemed a crass invasion of Americanism; together with dental floss and the word "period" to signal the end of a sentence (as opposed to menstrual flow or a segment of time).

"But it isn't so I can't. It's all you. Full stop."

Bernice pulled upon her synthetic cigarette in the small coffee shop, making no effort to speak quietly. The synthetic cigarette wasn't to help her stop smoking, it was just to allow her to smoke indoors or amongst children.

"You're so boring."

Bernice let the statement hang in the quiet air of the coffee shop – the Coffee Bean or whatever is was called. Conversations were halted mid-sentence. Newspapers were held but not read. The whiff of a "scene" was in the air and everyone wanted to partake. I could sense my fellow patrons waiting with bated breath for my response; tears, anger, anything of that sort. Perhaps a crumple of humiliation. They were all willing me to fly into a jilted fury. Anything that might constitute an anecdote.

I've learnt over the years to fake upset and disappointment when being dumped. It's the customary reaction and I've found that the dumper fails to get the sufficient level of closure on the dumping without some tearing of sackcloth or gnashing of teeth from the dumpee.

"He cried at first but took it OK in the end."

"He was pretty angry but he calmed down after a while."

"He was crushed. He's a broken man, emotionally crippled, eternally broken hearted. I never knew I could make a man love me so much."

These sorts of statements had a more authentic ring of truth to them when being reported back to new boyfriends or best friends or mutual acquaintances. Better than:

"He was fine actually, he just kept smiling."

I had intended to deploy my usual array of reactions when Bernice broke the news (I had become particularly adept at the single tear emanating from the right eyeball) but the allegation of "boringness" confounded me somewhat and I forgot myself.

"You think I'm boring?" I asked.

"Yes. Boring."

"But…"

"You think you're interesting because you see interesting plays and you watch interesting films. You read interesting books and you even know some interesting people who say interesting things. You think that makes you interesting. But it doesn't because you yourself never actually say or do anything interesting."

I opened my mouth to say something interesting but I got cut off.

"That's why people call you Second Hand Scott, because you're second hand. You live through other people. You never say or do anything original."

I was going to say something original…

"And besides, you only ever say nice things. You don't criticise. You don't antagonise. You don't moan. You don't argue. You don't even insinuate. And that Scott, is really very boring."

I had a flashback to evening after evening of sitting around Bernice's mother's kitchen table listening and smiling as Bernice and her creator dissected their common acquaintances with sweeping statements and crass generalisations. Their misguided attempts at psychoanalysis were astonishing.

And they classed this as "interesting" chat.

If someone showed cleavage they had self-esteem issues or borderline nymphomania. If someone showed no cleavage they were sexually repressed and pre-disposed to self-harm. If someone had their hair cut they had an anxiety disorder. If someone didn't have their hair cut they had intimacy issues. Bernice and her mother could read a debilitating personality defect into any situation.

"That Curry girl is pregnant and doesn't know who the father is. She's been putting it about a bit." Bernice's mother supplied the factual basis.

"Well, she wants to be loved and she's confused sexual union with relational intimacy. I imagine it's the freckles. They're so obvious."

"What do you think Scott?"

They turned expectantly to me through the haze of smoke and bad wishes. They wanted some fresh, malevolent impetus. I didn't really know what to say. Since Sally Paxton, I had tried never to be mean or hurtful to anyone. I steered clear of all Home Truths. I actively avoided Telling It As It Is. Besides, I had never met the Curry girl. I didn't even know if she had freckles. And I wasn't entirely sure of the Freckles-Promiscuity Matrix Theory so couldn't quite bring myself to endorse it.

"Ah, the exuberance of youth," I giggled.

They rolled their eyes at my inanity and seemed to make an unspoken agreement to leave me out of any future conversations – for which I was grateful.

Back in the coffee shop, Bernice was sucking furiously on her fake cigarette, the angry red tip mirroring the contentious look on her brow. She was challenging me, daring me, to dispute her carefully considered character assassination.

"You're just a bit bland Scott. Boring. Dull. Blank. Pleasant. In fact, you're so nice; you're virtually sexless."

Project #1 – Sally Paxton (the definition of unsuccessful – as in dead)

Hello. Hola. Buongiorno.

My name is Scott. Scott Nathaniel Logan if you want to be formal. But people call me Second Hand Scott. It's a nickname I've had since secondary school, when my mum was spotted buying some clothes in a charity shop. This ingenious and witty nickname became embedded across the entire school within a week. Accompanied by…

"Your shoes used to be owned by a paedo."

"Those pants are probably full of a tramp's pubic lice."

"What do you spend all your money on then – spring rolls and chow mein?"

I just smiled and laughed where appropriate; scratching my groin occasionally to get in on the joke. Even the attempt at a racial slur didn't bother me – mainly owing to the fact that I'm not Chinese. It is true, I do have a slight (really very slight) oriental look about my features but, alas, there is not even a hint of exotic blood within me. My family, drawn mainly from East Anglia, are somewhat bemused by my (really barely noticeable) Mandarin features. Some suspicion did fall upon my mum in my early years; many of our relatives wondering aloud if number 47 was the only thing my mum ordered from Mr Wings, the local Chinese restaurateur.

So, by the time I was labelled "Second Hand Scott" I was already pretty accustomed to a derogatory nickname or two. "Chinese Scott" was one. "The Chink" was another favourite. (The school I went to wasn't particularly enlightened; socio-politically speaking). Before that I was "Potato Boy" or "Scampi" or "Fishcake" because my family ran (and still run) a fish and chip shop. The "Ballroom Dancing Wanker" was another one – for reasons which are self-explanatory.

"I bet your mum buys stuff from charity shops so she can spend all her money on Chinese lady boys," those witty little scamps from school would say.

I just kept smiling throughout and admitted quite freely that my mum probably was partial to the odd oriental trans-gender prostitute and that yes, she did shop in the British Heart Foundation from time to time.

The "time to time" part was a subtle lie. My mum bought almost everything from charity shops, discount stores or via the free ads in the local newspaper. Even some of my Christmas and birthday presents had that tell-tale "worn" look. Indeed, almost everything in our house had been "pre-loved." I didn't mind. (I mind very little). I came to see a kind of beauty in it I suppose. When we studied the Second World War in the third year of secondary school, I found that we, as a family, were just perpetuating that wartime spirit of "make do and mend." (That's what I told myself anyway).

It wasn't that we were tight fisted, we just genuinely didn't have anything. Well, not much anyway. My parents were (and still are) restaurateurs of the takeaway variety. Despite the shop being extremely popular and well thought of in the locality, it never actually seemed to make any money. After achieving a high grade in my Business Studies GCSE exam, I did suggest to my father (utilising all my recently acquired economic acumen) that he might like to increase his prices once in a while, the last increase in the price of saveloy coming in the late 1990s. But he just stared at me until I went away.

For a year or two I wondered if my father might be stockpiling a huge surplus of profit for my benefit. As a boy, I had a recurring daydream of my father presenting me with a brand new Ferrari on my eighteenth birthday, bought from his secret excesses of wealth. I used to wonder if he had opened a secret bank account for me where he was carefully depositing all the riches of the lucrative takeaway food market. One day he would present me with a gold card that would hold the key to my every dream, whim and desire. He would say to me, "Son, I haven't bought a new pair of trousers in fifteen years so I could bequeath every penny I've earned to you. My life has been boring, quiet and ordinary. I want yours to be exciting, loud and extraordinary. Drive fast cars. Make love to beautiful women. Get tattoos that would shame your mother. Check into rehab from time to time. Just *live* boy." But those dreams never became a reality (for my eighteenth birthday my father gave me a blue watch that I know for certain had been left behind in the shop a few months before) and I came to the conclusion that whilst my father could fry with the best of them, he didn't really know how to run a business.

I don't remember either of my parents having any extravagances. They certainly didn't deprive me in order to indulge themselves. My father didn't drink or smoke. He wasn't exciting enough to have a gambling addiction or to visit Ladies of the Night. My mum didn't buy expensive perfume or glossy magazines. And she wasn't interesting enough to spend more than she should on alcohol or to subsidise a lazy lover (Chinese lady boy or otherwise) somewhere across town. They didn't make much and they didn't spend much. And I had to play by the same rules. The only unnecessary expenditure incurred for my benefit was a weekly cheque to the Happy Feet Dance School.

I just accepted it. (I accept a lot).

So, the ritual bullying of the school playground never really got to me: it prompted neither embarrassment nor shame; the lifeblood of adolescent victimisation. The jibes quickly fell away. But, unfortunately, the name remained. So, Second Hand Scott I became.

I just smiled it out.

I'm surprised I never got the nickname "Smiler" or "Smiley Scott" or something like that. I smile a lot – it's my inescapable dominant facial characteristic. It's the default expression of my visage. Many of my relatives assumed I was gormless or retarded in my early years; such was my incessant smiley-ness. Sitting in poo, smeared in food, being scolded by an angry parent – I would happily gurn through any situation.

In fact, I smile so much that some people find it offensive. The same people who find good moods on a Monday morning grating. The same people who deem whistling a crime worthy of capital punishment. My face has a natural plumpness to it and that somehow manages to make me look jovial, and ever so slightly oriental, without even meaning to.

"What are you so happy for?"

People would often scowl at me on the train; in a lift; in a queue; anywhere in response to my habitual grin.

It's funny how people assume that if you smile a lot you are, by definition, a happy person. (As if superficial smiley-ness automatically excludes subterranean sadness). The two are linked I suppose but that's not to say one can't happen without the other. Ask Sally Paxton. (Well, you can't. She's dead).

Home was a fish and chip shop called "Fry Days." It's on a long busy street and is successful enough to cause significant parking issues on a Friday and Saturday evening. My parents became quite familiar with Mr Lamb, the local Council's Transport Strategy Officer. He was a frequent visitor, incensed that deep fried foodstuffs could cause a major block to one of the town's main vehicular arteries. Keeping traffic moving was his passion. If anyone visiting the town praised its infrastructure within his hearing he would be orgasmic with delight. For a carefully considered transport strategy to be foiled by the cheap fare of a tacky takeaway with a neon sign drove him mad. He took early retirement when my father branched out into kebabs.

We lived above and behind the shop; the living space of what could have been quite an attractive terraced townhouse compressed significantly by the deep fat fryers and the potato peeler.

Home, the commercial façade and the residential rear, was neither a happy nor an unhappy place for me as a child. It was just busy. My father had only two days off per year in all my childhood. Christmas Day and Boxing Day. Every other single day of the year he would twist the little red and white sign on the front door of the shop at exactly midday; ready for business. That sign wouldn't be interfered with until after eleven at night. For those hours our lives would be beholden to the bell above the front door. That noise cut across anything and everything – familial entertainment, maternal affection, paternal scoldings; nothing could stand in its way.

"Mouths to feed," my father would say as he abandoned whatever lay in front of him at the time; be it the daily paper, a dirty nappy or my mum; legs akimbo. (As if).

My father didn't even close the shop on the occasion of his father's funeral. He just put a sign on the door saying "Open from 3."

My mum allowed herself the rather extravagant amount of seven days holiday per year. In addition to the two days my father took she also allowed herself a five day holiday in Blackpool where we stayed with my Auntie Pamela, a morose spinster who hated Blackpool and all its garish trappings. She seemed to hate it when we visited too – forcing her, as we did, to endure the agony of a trip to the sands, the torture of a promenade along the pier and the prolonged torment of a trip to the Tower Ballroom. But we went and enjoyed it (excepting Auntie Pam of course) because Blackpool, as my mum told me, was the Home Of Dance.

The rest of the year I spent in the shop: taking orders, throwing potatoes into the vast peeling machine and trying to flirt with the female customers (when I was old enough). My diet consisted of leftovers. My sleeping place was often whichever vacant shiny surface I could find. My toys consisted mainly of polystyrene cups (for peas, beans, gravy and curry sauce) and little polystyrene plates (for almost everything else) perhaps with a few plastic forks thrown in for variety. I used to make little polystyrene friends out of them.

Every Friday evening my mum would take me to a converted warehouse about half a mile away from our house and make me dance with a succession of bossy girls with extremely tight pony tails. My mum wanted me to be a dancer. I have no idea why. I don't think she ever danced as an adult or as a child. She showed very little interest in dancing and she generally looked bored when we went to the Tower Ballroom. She wouldn't even stay to watch me dance on a Friday evening. She would drop me off at five o clock and be back at six on the dot to take me home. She never let me miss a lesson.

That was my childhood in a nutshell. Some would call it idyllic; others would say boring as hell. At the very least, it was innocent and carefree and rather quiet. Until Sally Paxton died of course. And when I say "died" I mean "murdered."

Project #15 – Wendy the Worst (successful / non-successful is not the right matrix)

After the excitement and stress of Projects 13 and 14, I had a bit of a fallow period. My Projects tend to have a way of running into each other; one would often overlap into the next. But after Joan (Project #14), I couldn't get a sniff. I am not good in such situations; I feel purposeless, obsolete, lacking in direction. Bored even. So, I moped about a bit and took a long walk by the sea whilst thinking about Sally Paxton (deceased) before deciding to get back down to work.

I decided to join a choir in order to encounter some female company. This is what I do. I make decisions that result in me doing things (for short periods of time) in the hope of meeting girls. I joined a mountaineering club once. I did a floristry course. I went to a series of lectures about hedgehogs. I joined a book club; the gramophone society; the Church of Latter Day Saints. All in the hope of meeting girls. (Some were more successful than others).

In fact, I joined two choirs to maximise my chances of meeting a girl in need of a boy.

The first choir was a choral group at work. It was fairly high brow. They sang posh sounding pieces and used sentences like "this is classic Baroque" or "the Romantic period, with Chopin at the forefront, created some beautiful works for collective voice." I had no idea what they were talking about but I smiled a lot, nodded occasionally, and they seemed to be happy with that. I'd seen the advert on the notice board at work and thought I'd give it a spin. It may not be the classic refuge of a recently jilted girl – the gym or the pub are much more common – but you never know...

The choral group, rather accurately named "The Work Choir", met in meeting room 4D on a Tuesday lunchtime. I went along that first week with some trepidation. Not about the potential public audition that I might face – why would I be embarrassed about that when I spent much of my childhood in sequins? – but about what might lay ahead on the girl-front. I felt that I was building to something. Something really worthy.

That long walk by the sea had given me the time to think.

I got the opportunity to reflect upon my life to date; especially as my thirtieth birthday had just passed without much fanfare. I got a card from my mum of course, purchased from the local open air market. And two days after my birthday I got a text from Dave (my "best" mate since school) saying, "Happy Birthday knobhead. Hope you got some chopsticks" but other than that, it was all fairly low key. I had spent the actual day alone. I did flick through my little black book to see if any of the various girls I'd met over the years might be available to perhaps join me for a meal, but there wasn't anyone really.

That clear coastal air blew in and out of my brain, allowing me to think clearly. My life had been what some people might call wasted. I had a university degree that I had never used. I was still "temping" in various office suites around town. I had no car, no mortgage, no golf clubs. I had considerable latent ballroom dancing talent, entirely unharnessed. I had a website that was still active but which only amassed thirteen or fourteen hits a year. I had no girlfriend. Indeed, I had contributed, quite significantly, to the death of Sally Paxton – my very first girlfriend.

And the raison d'etre of my life...my restoration Projects...weren't all that impressive either. Who had I helped? Who had I actually helped...? Really...?

But still, I had a feeling that the next Project would be worthwhile. It was to be a defining project of restoration. Someone would be changed for the better, I could feel it. So I joined the choir.

When I arrived at meeting room 4D there were three old men and four older women, milling around, waiting, chatting, edging towards death. As I walked through the door, their eyes didn't light up in a "oh-here-is-a-potential-young-new-member-of-our-rather-old-fashioned-choral-choir-let's-be-nice-to-him..." way. No, their eyes seemed to say, "don't-get-excited-we've-been-here-before-he's-probably-looking-for-another-room."

"Is this the Work Choir?" I asked.

"It is. Can we help you?"

"Yes, I've come to sing."

They just blinked at me. Collectively. For a long, long time.

"Are we waiting for the others?" I ventured into the geriatric torpor.

One of the old ladies, with a scrunched up little face, shook off the lethargy.

"This is it. We're all here."

Even my relentless happy optimism shrunk a little in the face of those seven old age pensioners. There was not a project amongst them. (Please God, let there not be a project amongst them. I couldn't face another Kay (Project 10)). But then, I thought...perhaps one of their granddaughters might be in distress. A great-niece might be prohibitively ugly. A family friend might be about to denounce men for all eternity due to an encounter with the local cad or bounder. I could help.

"There's a lovely young man who sings with us at work. Beautiful vocal chords. He'll take you for a drink without trying to put his hand up your top."

I thought I'd give it a whirl...

"We're just waiting for Wendy."

"And who is Wendy?" I ventured, hoping beyond hope that the rather old fashioned name might be attached to some young recently jilted temptress in need of an accommodating young man to bring back her inner confidence through frequent and passionate sexual union. Or similar.

"She is our leader," said one.

"Our choirmaster," said another.

"Hitler," said an old man at the back.

"More like Genghis Khan. At least Hitler was nice to animals," piped up another wrinkly.

I did a little nervous giggle, assuming this to be a geriatric joke of sorts. "Is she nice?"

"No she is not nice," a booming voice came from the doorway.

I turned to confront...Wendy.

Wendy was younger than I had anticipated. Really quite young. Her hair was brown and centrally parted. Her body was slim, although her shoulders were quite broad, giving her a rather V shaped aspect. Her skin looked decent, although besmirched by the odd mole here and there. She stood bolt upright and lifted her chin, thrusting her generous bosom into the world. Her clothes were on the functional side but of good quality and in relatively good taste. As a package, she passed muster.

But her face. Oh my.

It had all the right features and in all the right proportions...but...well, she wasn't ugly exactly, she was just stern. Well, not just stern. Really, really, stern. It was stamped all across her face (and stamped with a really heavy stamp). Even in the throes of orgasmic pleasure she would no doubt look like she was about to dismember you. (Pardon the pun). Hitler Smitler – I bet even he smiled from time to time. Wendy scared the bejesus out of me within a second.

"She is not nice. She is not friendly. She is not in the business of choral creativity to make friends." Wendy spoke about herself in the third person which, in my limited experience, immediately marks someone out as a twat. "Who are you?"

"My. Name. Is. Scott."

She glared at me so strongly I found it difficult to speak. I could only manage one word in a sentence before clamming up.

"Are you here to sing?"

"Yes."

"Can you sing?"

"Erm..."

"I will make you sing."

She stalked into the room, flashing her eyes around the assembled choristers.

"Where is Gerald?" she demanded.

"Dead."

"Oh my God," she shouted towards the heavens, cursing the loss of a dear old soul. (Or so I thought; she was actually cursing the loss of a mediocre tenor).

"The liver finally gave way."

"Boring. Not interested. I am interested only in the living. I am interested only in singing. Put Gerald out of your mind. Good riddance. He's dead to me now."

"He is dead to all of us," ventured the same brave old man in a rather factually accurate manner.

"That's the spirit. Now, let's sing."

By the time I got back to my desk after lunch, I was exhausted. I had gone twelve rounds with a choral dictator and had been comprehensively beaten, excoriated and eviscerated. Wendy was just really, really mean. I had never met anyone so unrelentingly horrible. She didn't smile. She didn't compliment or praise. And she did not hold back in her constructive criticism. When Albert sang a duff note she called him a tone deaf word-that-my-mum-wouldn't-like-me-to-say. When Hilary started to cough whilst Wendy was delivering firm instructions, Wendy smacked the old bird as hard as she could on the back. (I thought I heard something crack but was too scared to say anything). Half way through learning an aria I started to suspect that my fellow singers might not be old age pensioners at all – they might well have been people my own age who had been subjected to the relentless barrage of Wendy for a month or two. Like a deep sea fisherman being battered by a coarse salt water wind; they looked old and withered and scored.

As we shuffled out of the room in disgrace…"In my eighteen months as creative director of this choral group I have never been so embarrassed by the sheer ineptitude of its members"…I asked Albert why everyone didn't leave and join a choir where you might get some respect and / or some refreshments. (The absence of physical assault was the least you could ask for, surely. If not, some biscuits would be something). Albert just laughed and laughed some more as he shuffled off down the corridor.

I subsided into my chair and took a deep breath.

I had never met anyone like Wendy. She was corrosive.

Chapter 2

"Jealous"

Project #5 – Jenny the Jealous (Unsuccessful, or possibly successful, depending on how you look at it)

In the first year of university (yes, I got in to one!) I met a girl called Jenny (although it took me quite a while to actually find out her name. She had simulated sex on me before I found out what was on her birth certificate). She was gorgeous. Blonde, thin, high cheek bones, the classic head turning look.

"Do you know any magic?" she said to me when we first met.

We were at a house party. I have no idea whose house it was or whether I had actually been invited there. But I was there and I walked round looking for girls, and helping myself to whatever food and drink I could find – as students do.

Jenny had caught my attention fairly quickly, what with her striking blonde hair and her rather jazzy sense of style – a hat at a jaunty angle, a scarf carelessly but perfectly positioned across her shoulder, trouser legs of differing lengths.

"Afraid not," I replied, trying to hint as I did that I might have other dextrous and intriguing "talents."

"Good, it's overrated anyway."

"I agree."

(It is my policy to agree with girls as often as possible – they seem to like it).

"Just cheap tricks," this girl, Jenny, said with a fair degree of feeling.

"I agree wholeheartedly. I struggle to remember whether David Copperfield is a character from a Dickens' novel or a person who can make the Statue of Liberty disappear."

As I spoke, I found I was almost boring myself, and decided that it might be a good time to leave. Playful, witty repartee had never been my forte and Jenny didn't look the type to put up with such inane drivel; the jocularity of her wardrobe was quite at odds with the crease on her brow and the tightness of her mouth. Besides, she was too attractive for all that nonsense. Good looking girls can't abide bad conversation I've found. So I thought I'd head off before she told me to sod off. But just at that moment, a handsome man with a shaved head and a pack of (magical) cards in one hand walked past, leading a very attractive blonde haired girl with the other. He glanced our way. Jenny chose that moment to kiss me suddenly and forcefully on the mouth. She also grabbed me under through my trousers, which was an unexpected treat. After a moment or two she released my appendage and my lips and said, "Ha! What do you think of that?"

I thought she had been speaking to me so I said, "Very nice thank you," but it turned out she'd been speaking to the peripatetic magician who'd just walked past. He'd gone though, so he probably didn't hear or see.

Jenny left me without a backward glance.

I saw her a few weeks later at a nightclub. (She was wearing leather trousers). I danced near to her for a bit and tried to catch her eye, pulling out all the seductive moves I'd learnt at the Happy Feet Dance School. She didn't spare me a glance. She was trying to dance near the magician with the shaven head and catch his eye, but he didn't spare her a glance either even though she was bouncing her bosoms in his vicinity for all she was worth. The magician was gyrating against anything in his path, whether it caught his eye or not. He even thrust his groin in my direction once, perhaps having been disorientated by some inopportune strobe lighting. I parried his groinal thrust with one of my own and he turned his attention elsewhere.

Eventually, Jenny gave up trying to entice the shaven headed magician and headed to the bar with a sad face; perhaps to give her boobs a rest. I followed and smiled at her until she was obliged to talk to me.

"Can I help you?" she said without in any way appearing helpful.

"It's Scott."

"Who is?"

"Me Is. I mean, I am. I'm Scott."

"And who are you?"

"We met a few weeks ago. We shared an intimate moment of a penal nature. Do I mean penal? That's something to do with prisons isn't it? I meant something pertaining to or relating to the penis."

She walked off about half way through my first sentence; somewhere in the region of "penal."

I made a note to myself to stop trying to engage girls in discussions about semantics in busy night clubs. Or indeed, anywhere.

Having taken note of that note-to-self, I decided to give it another go with Jenny.

I found her standing on the first floor of the nightclub. She was looking over the balcony down on to the dance floor. She looked sad. I joined her and smiled.

"You're a bit creepy," she said without looking at me.

"Am I?"

"You just keep following me around and you don't say much. And you're smiling."

"I like smiling."

"What is there to smile about?"

She hadn't taken her eyes off the dance floor below. It took me only a second to find the magician, locked in a passionate embrace with something blonde.

"Do you know martial arts?" Jenny asked.

"No."

"I thought all Chinese people knew martial arts?"

"I'm not Chinese."

"Shame."

"Why?"

"I just thought you might be able to beat someone up for me."

"Sorry. I'm a pacifist. I don't..."

And she walked off.

A few hours later I somehow found myself behind her in the taxi queue, which did seem fairly creepy I'll admit. (It was unintentional this time). The magician was at the front of the queue with another blonde girl on his arm. It may have been the same one from the dance floor or it may have not, it was hard to tell. They jumped into the next available taxi as Jenny watched on. I thought I heard a sob catch in her throat although it could have been a squeak from her leather trousers.

She saw me and pulled me into the next available cab.

"I'm not taking you home for sex. I just want to halve the cost of the taxi," she said as soon as we got in.

"Understood. Whatever you need," I said, being the very image of the principled gentleman. "But if you change your mind..."

She seemed pre-occupied so I let her stare out of the window for a few moments. (A skill I'd learnt from my father when he had to deal with indecisive customers or with my mum).

"Who is that guy?"

"Which guy?"

"The magician. The guy with the shaved head. The guy with the blondes."

"Him? Oh...he's my fiancée."

"Your fiancée? But..."

"But he's shagging his way through the entire first year, I know."

"So, how...?"

"We have an open relationship."

"OK..."

There was an awkward silence, made all the more awkward by the taxi driver turning the radio down in a blatant attempt at eavesdropping. An open relationship...this sounded promising (for me).

"We've been together since we were fifteen. Childhood sweethearts. But he wanted to break up with me when we came to university. He said he wanted to live a little, otherwise he might regret it in later life. I said that was fine because I want to live a little too. I want to sow some wild oats and put it about a bit, I said."

"But you don't?" (Please say you do).

"No."

We sat in silence for a bit as I assigned Jenny Project Number 5.

"We're having an open relationship for the first year and then we'll go back to normal in the second year. Get it out of our systems."

"Sounds great."

"Yes, it is," she said in a very firm voice.

But then she started to cry and I tapped her knee in friendly condolence. The taxi driver shook his head in sympathy and added another thirty pence to the meter when he thought we weren't looking.

When I got into bed with her a few minutes later (fully clothed), she pushed her head into my chest and sobbed loudly - which made it absolutely clear to me that no sex was intended.

"The thing I really don't understand....is that he keeps sleeping with girls who look just like me," she said between sobs

As she fell asleep, I stroked her blonde hair for a bit and pondered.

I wondered how I could help her. Some sort of affirmative action was probably called for. An intervention. Maybe I could go and have a word with the magician, man to man. Maybe I could threaten him with physical violence. Maybe I could slip insulting notes under his door under cover of darkness. But no, none of that would actually help and at least one of them was likely to get me beaten up.

I was still thinking up imaginative ways to surreptitiously help Project Number 5 when I dropped off to sleep.

The next morning, Jenny was up bright and breezy, not a hint of a tear in her eye or a sob in her throat. She brought me a cup of tea in bed and started to engage me in normal conversation; entirely at odds with her rather brusque manner the night before. What school did I go to, what subject was I studying at university – that sort of thing. When I made a movement to leave, she raced off to the kitchen to make pancakes. She brought them through to me on a large padded tray, together with sugar, maple syrup and lemon juice. I had to work through about fifteen of the blighters before I could raise the subject of leaving once again.

I queried the whereabouts of my undergarments. (I was sure I had them on when I dropped off the night before. Indeed, I thought I had been fully clothed).

"Could you stay a few more minutes?" she pleaded as she ignored the question.

"Why?"

"Because...because Sebastian will be back soon and I'd quite like him to see you here. In my bed. With no clothes on."

So, without many thoughts towards my physical wellbeing, I stayed in that bed for another hour before Sebastian eventually wandered in. I steeled myself for a rowdy physical encounter as Sebastian attacked me in a fit of cuckolded passion. I was very clearly naked; I was quite nonchalantly lying in Jenny's bed with a padded tray on my lap and Jenny was quite brazenly straddling me (and the padded tray). (Although she only did that when she heard the front door). I was certain that Sebastian couldn't help but be enraged by the behaviour of his childhood sweetheart. But he just said, "morning Jenny, morning mate, I'm off for a shower. Hardly got a wink of sleep." (So that was her name).

When Jenny heard the shower go on, she started to cry again. I tried to put a sympathetic hand on her shoulder in further friendly condolence but she shrugged it off and asked me to leave.

A few days later Jenny collared me in the library and pulled me over to sit at her table. She made sure we were sitting close, thighs touching, when Sebastian walked in. He was friendly once more, "afternoon" he said, and went off to sit at a table populated entirely by blondes. (How did he manage to locate them?) Within a few moments it was obvious that he'd managed to distract one of them with the dexterity of his hands. (Not that I could see his hands...)

Jenny spent more time watching him than reading her books.

My heart broke for her. I certainly knew the pang of unrequited love. I knew the anguish of unfaithfulness. I resolved that I would do anything I could for poor Jenny. If she needed fleeting and occasional comfort, I would provide it. If she needed a male object to provide the illusion of relational gay abandon, I would be it.

I tried to tell her this but the librarian walked past at that moment and shushed me. All Jenny managed to catch was something about "gay abandon." But still, she eventually caught my meaning and smiled grimly.

"That's why they call you Second Hand Scott is it?" she said, but I wasn't really sure why.

I have never been a member of the Boy Scouts but, if I had, I would have been an exemplar. That whole first year of university I was prepared. I was *en guard* as they say. At any moment, Jenny could appear out of the ether and purloin me for use in some scheme designed to make Sebastian insanely jealous. (The "make someone jealous" badge).

"Just talk to me and look interested."

"Laugh really loudly, now."

"Say you like my boobs."

But it didn't work. Sebastian didn't bat an eyelid. Perhaps he was relieved that Jenny had embraced the concept of the open relationship too. Perhaps it absolved him of any guilt. Perhaps it spurred him on to greater and better and blonder things. Either way, my involvement was ultimately fruitless. Sebastian gallivanted through the nubile girls of the first year, Jenny watched on in frustration and regret and I just hung about – looking hopeful and gormless by equal measure. We just all kept doing what we were doing.

I don't know who was most desperate.

Project #1 – Sally Paxton (deceased)

My first crush was a German exchange student called Heidi. She was an athletic Amazonian goddess, sun-kissed and toned. She was only at our school for a week – before heading for the Jurassic Coast – but I was besotted. She probably didn't even know my name though. (She may have even thought I was a fellow exchange student – having flown in from China). I only watched her from afar, not quite having the courage to talk to her. Before I knew it, she was gone.

My second love was a geography teacher whose name I can't even remember. She always wore high heels and red nail varnish which somehow contrived to make geography the most erotic lesson on the timetable. My third love was...who knows? I think I loved twelve different females throughout Secondary

School, including the strange looking Indian dinner lady who once ruffled my hair as I waited in line for Macaroni Cheese. And my unrequited loves at the Happy Feet Dance School must have been bordering on triple figures. I would fall in love every time I changed partner. The more severe the pony tail the more fierce my love, my devotion, my jealousy, my obsession.

Not one of them loved me back.

I wasn't bad looking. I had (and have) a certain floppy charm. And my body was and is slim and quite firm in places. That was a little bit of a surprise owing to all the fried food I would eat at home. But thanks must go to a fast metabolism and to all that dancing my mum made me do. I was clean. My ears didn't stick out and my hair was quite nicely cut due to a convenient services swap arrangement with the hairdressers next door to my father's shop. I didn't smell unduly of fried food. Well, if I did, no-one ever said. And bearing in mind that they used to call me the "Chinese-looking-cha-cha-cha-deep-fried-dickhead" at school, I don't think they would have held back had I faintest whiff of a saveloy about me. I was alright.

But still, it was always me doing the loving.

I loved them all. Or thought I did. Until I met Sally Paxton of course. (That's when I found out what real love is. And it's not just a lovely warm feeling. It's thorny and dark).

"I've got a girlfriend," I said with as much feigned casual, off the cuff, spontaneous nonchalance as I could muster. (Which may have been over the top). I lounged in a chair in the kitchen of my childhood home and tried to act as if this kind of thing was run of the mill for me whilst secretly hoping that my parents would whoop in delight and perhaps book a venue for the wedding.

My father just stared at me, diverting his eyes away from the local paper for a moment or two.

My mother smiled and said, "of course you have dear."

Project #15 – Wendy the Worst (the worst)

My second choir of the day was about as different to the first as it could be. It was in a pub for a start. There were young people there who seemed to be enjoying themselves. And they were singing songs that I had heard of.

A tall bloke with a goatee greeted me at the door. He was wearing a t-shirt with "Funk Soul Family" emblazoned across it. He shook my hand. His palm was quite wet.

"Welcome Funk Soul Brother," he said.

"Hello," I said.

He put his hand on my stomach and stared deep into my eyes.

"I can feel the song within you. Do you feel it?"

I empathised with many a pregnant woman as I said, "I suppose I do," in a squeaky, embarrassed, scared, uncomfortable, little voice. My jittery eyes flitted between his intense stare and his invasive hand.

"If you have the song, we have the funk. I'm going to put that funk in you. Please grab a drink, we'll be starting soon."

I wandered in – dazed and confused – and found myself at the bar. A man had just touched my *midriff* in a very intimate manner and promised to put some funk in me. A *man* had just touched my midriff in a very intimate manner and promised to put some funk in me. A man had just touched my midriff in a very intimate manner and promised to put some *funk* in me. Whichever way I said it, it felt weird. (And not in a good way). It took me a while to realise that a girl was trying to speak to me.

"Hello."

"Hello."

"Hello."

I finally heard her voice and turned my eyes outwards. And

I'm glad I did. She was pretty. Not conventionally pretty. She was a bit too toothy and a tad too spotty to turn heads or to elicit wolf whistles from big bottomed builders, but there was definitely something about her. She looked pleasant. That was it. Dark haired and slightly swarthy but most definitely pleasant. She looked like the kind of girl who might help in the community. She looked like the kind of girl who might care about the environment or might genuinely be concerned about people in Africa. There was a friendliness and simplicity about her that was attractive. She just seemed to radiate agreeability; and I was instantly taken with it. (Or it might have been her body, which was unbelievable).

I don't believe in love at first sight. Lust at first sight most definitely exists. (I have been afflicted by it for many years). I think I combined the two at that moment and found myself somehow in "luve."

"Are you alright?" she asked.

"A man has just touched my stomach and stared deep into my eyes," I said with a fair degree of feeling. (I couldn't help it, it just came out).

"That's Neil. He does that a lot. Sorry about that."

That made me feel better. She had that way about her, apologising for things that weren't her fault. And her eyes were slightly larger than normal eyes. They seemed to suggest she was interested in you. Or that she wanted to go to bed with you – depending on how horny the beholder was. (The "luve" was growing). Just as I was about to respond and say something charming to this pleasant creature, I heard some fearsome stomping. Someone (or something) was approaching the room.

"Don't touch my stomach dickhead."

Wendy stormed into the room and, within a moment, was at my side. Neil was left in her wake, unsure what to do with his wet hand and Wendy's allotment of Funk.

"Ah, Scott, is it? What are you doing here? Doesn't matter. Not interested. Buy me a drink. Vodka and coke please."

My hand was in my pocket before I even realised it.

I turned to the not classically attractive, tremendously pleasant looking girl to offer her a drink and realised that I didn't even know her name.

"Erm…would you…?"

"Fleur doesn't drink. She is a boring person." Wendy told me in strong, commanding terms.

Wendy and Fleur (what a beautiful name) were not looking at each other.

"I do drink. Just not to excess," Fleur told me. "Thank you Scott. I will have a glass of red wine. That's very kind of you. Rioja please."

Fleur smiled at me – which was ace. (Ace!) Wendy's face tightened – which was not.

"I will also have a glass of wine. Cancel my order of a vodka and coke. I will have a cabernet sauvignon Scott. That is also red wine. Large."

Wendy did not smile at me.

I ordered the drinks. I even got one for myself. I felt compelled to have a glass of red wine also, even though I had never really drunk red wine before (and when I did it had coca cola in it). Silence reigned behind me.

As I handed the drinks out, Wendy put her hand on my arm. Her grip was tight.

"Fleur, would you excuse us? I need to speak to Scott about urgent choral business. You are aware that I run another choir. A highly successful work based vocal collective. I only attend this one to remember what it is to be a part of a non-descript crowd rather than a dynamic and charismatic leader. It helps me empathise with my vocal flock. Scott is our newest recruit. I have to deliver feedback on his poor performance this afternoon."

"I think we're just about to start. Louis is here," Fleur responded.

"That diva will have to wait."

"OK, fine."

Fleur headed off, somewhat reluctantly, looking at her watch. I willed her to glance back at me but she didn't. (That's what girls do in the movies to signal sexual attraction). I turned my attention back to Wendy. She stared at me. Hard.

"You will have noted the sexual tension between Fleur and I."

I hadn't (although I did notice her poor grammar).

"I made a pass at Fleur a few months ago. She rebuffed me. You'll probably think she's a frigid whore."

I didn't. (Frigid and a whore…how?)

"As do I."

I smiled. I didn't know what else to do.

"She clearly has untapped sexual and sensual desires but she's not willing to discover them. I offered to assist. As an experienced and well-used bisexual I am fully qualified to plumb her depths, psychologically speaking. She rejected my offer. As I said, Fleur is a boring person."

I kept smiling.

"I'll level with you Scott. I'm not used to being rejected. I'm used to getting my own way. I don't like to be rebuffed unless that happens to be a sexual euphemism. To put it bluntly, I need a boyfriend to make me feel better. And it might as well be you."

The smile almost slipped.

I have done some things in my time. I have taken on some truly horrible Projects but I had a feeling that this was going to be the worst. Most the women I had encountered had something going for them; some were even nice. But I couldn't find one redeeming feature within Wendy. Even her love of singing seemed to be some sort of vanity.

And in the distance I could see Fleur. She was chatting to Neil, the wet palmed bearded pervert. I was consumed with immediate and furious jealousy. I hadn't had that feeling since Sally Paxton. I wanted to hurt Neil. I wanted to knock the funk out of him before he could try and put it in Fleur. Fleur saw me staring and smiled at me. Smiled at me. A nice smile. It calmed me down and I put aside any murderous thoughts towards Neil.

That was the kind of girl I would like.

(That was odd...I realised that I hadn't had a thought like that for a long time).

"Well, what of it?" demanded Wendy. "Will you take me on? I desperately need a boyfriend. I have needs that I require you to satisfy. Will you be my boyfriend?"

Conditioning. Mental conditioning. Years of adopting horrible, unlovable or broken girls. Piecing them together, building them up, letting them walk all over me, and then setting them free to love and be loved. All because I killed Sally Paxton without meaning to. That's what led me to say "Yes."

Wendy instantly turned round, clapped her hands and demanded the attention of the room. The Funk Soul Brothers and Sisters turned towards me.

"Quiet please. Everyone listen. I have an announcement. Fleur, are you listening? This is important. Scott and I have just become an item. He is now my lover and my companion. If any of you other ladies were interested in him, including you Fleur, it is too late. He is now officially off limits. He's mine until I decide to let him go."

At that moment, Wendy turned round, grabbed my head with both hands and crushed her face into mine – lips first. Her hands were clamped against my ears but I could just about hear someone mutter "poor sod" as I was physically assaulted.

Over the back of Wendy's head I could just see Fleur. She smiled wryly at me. I tried to make a "i-have-no-idea-what-is-happening-to-me-don't-let-this-affect-out-flegling-physical-attraction" gesture with me eyes but I'm not sure it communicated.

Wendy released me.

"Sod the singing. Let's go. I have to have you."

Chapter 3

"Silence"

Project #6 - Ellie-May the Elective Mute (I'm going to say…successful)

In all honesty, I shouldn't really classify Ellie-May as a Project…in that she didn't want or need help and, indeed, I didn't really give her any. The Project was all of her own making. I did go out with her though (after a fashion), and she did give me a potential money making idea – so I thought I better mention her.

Jenny introduced me to Ellie-May at the start of the second year of university. I had bumped into Jenny at the cash point on the first Monday of term. I hadn't heard from her over the summer so wasn't sure whether our on-off relationship was on or off. She cleared that up right away.

"I won't be needing you this year Scott."

"Really?"

"Sebastian and I are back together; properly I mean."

"Exclusive?"

"That's the word. Exclusive. We're living together and it's better than ever."

"Congratulations."

"Thank you. And thanks for everything. You really helped."

I don't think I had ever received thanks for my efforts. I was touched.

"I know I was quite horrible to you. And I didn't even give you any sex."

True, she had been horrible and also true, she hadn't offered any sex as a means of recompense for the horribleness. It would have softened the blow.

"I'm feeling a lot chirpier now so I'm more inclined to offer you some…"

Hello! He reapeth what he shall soweth.

"…but I can't because I'm in an exclusive, loving relationship."

Damneth.

As we had been chatting, a girl had sidled up behind us, waiting to withdraw cash. Jenny noticed her.

"Oh, hello Ellie-May."

Ellie-May nodded in polite greeting.

"Still at it then?"

Ellie-May nodded once again.

"You'll never make it you know."

Ellie-May smiled wryly.

"You're mad."

Ellie-May shrugged her shoulders and then nodded her head slightly in my direction. "Oh, sorry, Scott, this is Ellie-May."

"Hello," I said.

Ellie-May shook my hand.

"Pleased to meet you," I tried.

In response, Ellie-May nodded her head again; a rather formal greeting I thought.

"And how do you know each other?" I asked, starting my sentence with the word "and" in the pretence that a conversation actually existed.

At this point, Jenny started laughing.

"I think this is fate. You two hopeless cases were destined to meet each other. Ellie, this is Scott; the most docile, accepting and sexless individual I've ever met."

"Hang on a minute…" I began. (Sexless?) But I was cut off.

"Scott, this is Ellie-May, and she's a nymphomaniac."

Ellie-May shook her head vigorously. Jenny took the hint.

"Sorry. *Was* a nymphomaniac."

Ellie-May nodded and thrust her thumb over her shoulder, as if to say (but not actually to say) "yep, that's all in the past now, all that nymphomania."

"She regrets all that and has decided to become an elective mute for her second year at university."

"What's an elective mute?" I asked.

"Someone who decides not to talk."

"Why would someone do that?"

"You'll have to ask her."

"How?"

"You'll figure it out."

Jenny skipped away, giggling. Ellie-May and I stared at each other for a while. I waved, self-consciously. She waved, self-consciously. I smiled – wanly. She smiled – wanly. I raised my eyebrows. She raised her eyebrows.

It was like being with my father.

I mimed the prospect of having a drink; glugging away at an imaginary pint glass before realising that she was mute, not deaf.

"Would you like to go for a drink?"

She nodded and off we popped.

This being university, and it being just after midday, we immediately went to the Student Union and ordered a pint of lager each. (Well, I ordered them both actually). I had a hint of blackcurrant in mine to take the bitter edge off.

"So, you're an elective mute?" I said. "May I ask why?"

She didn't say anything.

"Can you give me a clue?"

Ellie-May pulled a notepad out of her pocket and started writing. As she did, I got a good look at her. She was rather petite, dark haired and not particularly attractive. (To my beholder at least). She was quite toothy and her nose was of a generous proportion. She was also wearing tremendously thick spectacles; the quintessential milk bottle bottoms.

She held her pad up to me.

"I did some things I regret – last year."

I had an idea what kind of things she was referring to. Sexual regret. It was the kind of regret sadly lacking from my life to date.

"How many things?" I asked.

More scribbling. "Sixty seven."

"Sixty seven? How on earth…?"

She wrote: "I get very sexy once I've had a few drinks."

I ordered more drinks.

"I recognise the need to change. That fourth S.T.D was persuasive."

I cancelled the drinks.

"Most of the men I slept with last year I didn't even want to sleep with. I just wanted people to like me. But no-one did. I need to change, to Find Myself…"

At this point I did wonder if I was being sucked into another homosexuality cover up (Carla – Project #4) (the capital letters being the big clue) and I had plenty of time to wonder as she was quite a slow writer.

"…I need to be confident in my own skin so I've decided to take a vow of silence for a year. I want to build myself from within."

I finished my drink, which went straight to my head, and found myself thinking of Sally Paxton. Poor old Sally Paxton, a girl desperate to be liked, craving the attention of men (or boys in Sally's case as we were at school) as a means of social affirmation. She bounced from one pre-pubescent boy to another; doing anything they asked of her in the hope of being "liked." Tragic really. I wondered if her path wasn't too different to that of Ellie-May.

"You're going to need help," I said.

Ellie-May raised an inquisitive eyebrow.

"If you're going to see this through, you'll need help. Someone to talk for you, someone to explain your situation, to be the voice of your inner desires. Like a guide dog that talks. I could help you with your Trappist vow of silence."

Scribbling.

"And Chastity."

Bugger.

But I'd said it now and if my father had taught me one thing it was that a man always keeps his word (singular in his case).

And so Ellie-May became my girlfriend - of sorts. Or perhaps I became her carer; I'm not quite sure – we never fully discussed or articulated the exact nature of our relationship. If I ever brought it up, her pen would somehow always run out of ink or the nib of her pencil would break or her notepad would fall out of the nearest open window.

In the first few weeks of being "together" quite a number of people asked me what was going on.

"Are you dating Ellie-May?"

"I thought you were called Second Hand Scott, not Seventy Second Hand Scott."

"We call her Ellie-Will, not Ellie-May, because she always will."

I baulked at this last one...as when he said "we" he was talking about the university Water Polo Team.

"Well not anymore," I said with wounded authority.

"More fool you then."

I puffed myself up with righteous indignation, the smile slipping from my face for a moment as I became a moralistic orator.

"I find your comments sexist and chauvinistic; as well as ill-informed. It is a hallmark of sexual prejudice to adversely judge an individual by their sexual history when that same standard is not applied universally..."

But he'd gone, probably to coax his horse into the swimming pool.

I came to know Ellie-May quite well across the year. I spent many a waking hour with her. And true to her word, Ellie-May never even hinted, via a suggestive eyebrow or an evocative elbow, at a potential sexual liaison. She remained steadfastly chaste and strictly silent. The closest she ever came to breaking her Trappist vow was when she stubbed her toe on a nest of tables. But the word that nearly escaped her lips, f-something, was never fully formed so I didn't count it against her.

In some ways I felt that I came to know her better than anyone I had ever known. An inclination of her head would tell me that she was in full agreement with me. A knitted brow would tell me that she was not. A head tilted one way would mean one thing; titled the other would mean another thing entirely. I could read her.

And in the unrelenting unresponsiveness, I was able to unload. I was able to talk; to really talk. To share my feelings; to express that which is within. My childhood. My parents' marriage. My doubts as to my sexuality in my ballroom dancing phase. Sally Paxton. I told her everything; revealing my inner sanctums.

It was cathartic, it was beautiful.

And yes, she did seem to find that inner peace, that sense of tranquillity that she had craved. Her brow un-furrowed, her shoulders un-tightened, her posture solidified. A new found sense of assurance seemed to grow on her. It was as if the very act of not talking, in a world full of noise, was the measure of defiance that allowed her to find her identity.

Obviously she never actually said that but I could read the signs. When we were together her eyes would often glaze over, as if she were looking inside herself. When I went to her house she would sometimes fail to answer the door, as if she were in such a deep phase of meditation that she couldn't rouse herself to allow me in. When I was telling her some interesting anecdote, she would often drop off to sleep - such was her state of utter contentment.

We were really quite intimate.

So it came as quite a surprise when her year was up, when the vow of silence expired, to hear Ellie-May's first words.

"Bugger me Scott, but you are boring. And if you mention Sally Paxton again I'll scream."

Ellie-May immediately told me a number of Home Truths; statements that had been burning a hole in her vocal chords for nearly a whole academic year. (And then she gave me a new business idea). She did admit that she could have written down the Home Truths for me but felt that it would be a waste of an angry rant which she was quite looking forward to. Besides, I had proved to be quite useful for answering telephones and asking for directions, etc and she didn't want me buggering off.

Firstly, she hated it when I called her Ellie-May because I somehow made it sound like she lived in a white painted wooden clapboard house in the mid-west plains of the United States. She didn't mind it from other people, even the university Lacrosse team who put quite a different emphasis on it, but from me she found extremely irritating.

Secondly, that Sally Paxton was dead and that it wasn't my fault and that I should just get over it. Or at least stop talking about it again and again and again.

Thirdly, she thought the only reason I kept going on about Sally Paxton was in a vain attempt to ascribe meaning to my boring, little life.

Fourthly, that she suspected that my mother wasn't happy in her marriage but that she didn't want to say more.

And lastly, that she thought I could start up a new business as a Professional Gooseberry.

This, of course, raised numerous questions...

"Professional Gooseberry? What's that?" I asked.

"Scott, let's face it, you're weird. You just smile all the time, regardless of the situation. You can just ignore all the awkwardness and tension around you. I have just insulted you a number of times and you've hardly batted an eyelid – you're just smiling as if it's all a joke. All the subtleties of life are completely lost on you. You'd be a perfect Professional Gooseberry."

So that was how I found myself sitting at a dinner table one evening surrounded by a bunch of people I had only just met together with a woman I had only met an hour or two before the others.

It turns out that I wasn't the only one to open my heart to the ever willing ear of Ellie during her year of silence. She was quite an attractive dumping ground for personal problems, private anxieties and delicate situations.

One of Ellie's lecturers had told Ellie, at length, about the break-up of her marriage. She had been "traded in for a younger model" a few months earlier; the bitterness of which cliché had not yet left her mouth. And now this lecturer was obliged to host the not-quite-ex-husband and his new girlfriend at a dinner party to celebrate the engagement of their only daughter. The presence of both parents was a necessity for such an occasion, even if they were accompanied by a large elephant. The lecturer couldn't bear the ignominy of having to host that dinner party as a singleton whilst her smug, middle aged, paunchy, balding husband grinned like a Cheshire cat who gets to have sex with a younger, slimmer, bigger breasted cat on regular occasions.

The occasion promised to be one of supreme awkwardness and barely suppressed rage. Ellie thought I'd be perfect for such an assignment. So she had put my name forward...

The lecturer, a Polish lady called Rachel, sat me down for a few minutes before the dinner party. I had arrived looking rather svelte and sexy, with a bunch of flowers and an understanding smile.

"So, we're agreed on £5 an hour. Try not to speak. If anyone asks you a question, let me answer it for you. Pretend your English isn't that good if you need to. If I say something funny, try to laugh. If I kiss you, kiss back. But otherwise don't do anything. OK?"

I smiled, nodded and thought, "wow, I'm getting paid for this!"

"So, Scott, where did you meet my ex-wife?" said the paunchy, balding husband, as he leaned back in his chair, swirling red wine.

Now, Ellie-May seemed to be of the opinion that the intricacies of human relational activity were beyond me…but that couldn't be further from the truth. I could sense tension in the air when it was indeed in the air. I had a very sophisticated niggle-ometer if I chose to turn it on. I was adept at reading subtext. It's just that sometimes, I chose not to read it.

Rachel, for example, was desperately trying to impress her ex-husband, his bit of stuff, and her daughter. She was trying to impress the ex-husband by showing considerable cleavage and laughing outrageously at every opportunity as if to say, "look how well I'm dealing with this." She was trying to impress the bit of stuff by sucking in her stomach and making the occasional lewd remark as if to say, "there is nothing sexier than a woman with a bit of experience under her belt." And she was trying to impress her daughter by being extremely polite and considerate to everyone and about everything as if to say, "this is how a gracious, confident woman acts in the face of provocation." The ex-husband was desperately trying to impress his bit of stuff, his ex-wife and his daughter by….well, I needn't get into that as long as you appreciate that I can analyse psychological and social intricacies as well as the next man.

All the while, the little bit of stuff looked bored, the daughter looked sick and the prospective son-in-law looked aghast. What on earth was he marrying into? Only I retained a sense of calm serenity but then again, I was the only one being paid.

"We met in the gym," said Rachel. "Scott has got a great body. A very tight bottom. I couldn't take my eyes off it."

"So you work out do you, Scott?" said the husband, father, lover, philanderer.

"He does indeed. A lovely flat stomach. Very sexy. Good for sitting on, if you know what I mean."

Rachel then roared with laughter at her own joke. No-one else did though, so Rachel flung back another glass of wine. I sipped my water. Rachel said that I wasn't to drink, mainly because she didn't want me making a mistake and giving her away. If anyone asked why I wasn't drinking, I was to say that my body was a temple or that it was frowned upon in China.

As the night progressed, the husband kept looking at me with suspicious eyes and plying me with questions. Rachel answered every single one on my behalf and the only questions I fielded on my own account were concerned with salt, pepper, gravy and more water. Every time Rachel left the room, I had to go with her, under the pretence of helping.

"How am I doing? How are we doing? Is it realistic? Am I doing OK? Is everyone having a good time? Do you think my daughter is OK, she looks pale? Is that girl attractive? Am I doing OK?" Rachel asked me in the kitchen, almost hyperventilating as she did, whilst I shaved some parmesan on to something.

"You're doing great. Everyone is having a great time," I said in my most reassuring, professional voice – virtually velveteen.

"Be quiet Scott. It's a car crash of an evening."

Project #1 – Sally Paxton (defunct)

"This girl that you're friendly with…" said my mum in a rather uncertain way.

"My girlfriend?" I asked.

"Well, yes, the girl you're friendly with."

I was sitting in the back of the shop on a rather sleepy Wednesday evening. I had been trying to get to grips with my homework; something about population spikes in East Asia, whilst my parents did all that was necessary to run an efficient and well thought of fish and chip shop (renowned for its cleanliness and hygiene standards I might add). However, the evening had been quiet and so my father was reading the local evening newspaper and my mum was fussing about; buffing surfaces that didn't need buffing and securing container lids that were already secure.

"What about her?" I asked, needing no excuse to distract myself from geography.

"Nothing really, I've just heard about her."

"Is it that thing that was in the newspaper a few years ago? They exaggerated it. Nothing actually burnt down..."

"No. Not that."

"Heard what then?"

My mum hesitated: "That she's a bit of a girl."

My father put down his newspaper and turned to face us; interested, for once, in his son's life. It seemed to unnerve my mum somewhat.

"And where have you heard that?" I said, rather tightly, removing the smile from my face.

"Just at the school gates, that's all," she said quickly.

A bit of a girl. A...bit...of...a...girl. I was incensed. I was enraged. A bit of a girl. The fact that it was true made it all the more infuriating.

"She's not like that," I said as firmly as I could to my dear old mum. "Anymore."

My father raised an eyebrow at my mum. She saw it. I saw it. She knew what it meant. I didn't.

"I just want you to be careful. I don't want you to get into any trouble. I don't want you to make the mistakes that..."

Even with my lack of emotional depth I could sense the tension in that room at that moment. It was palpable. It was in my mum's intake of breath. It was in the way my father moved in his chair. It was the kind of tension that usually only existed in our house-cum-shop on a Friday evening when I was getting ready to head out to the Happy Feet Dance School. It was so noticeable, and all the more incongruous, by the fact that my family home was usually filled with…well, nothing. My mum's hesitation was miniscule I suppose, but significant all the same.

"…others have made," finished my mum.

Project #15 – Wendy the Worst / Fleur the Finest (despair / hope)

"Would you like me to make a speech?" asked Wendy.

"Erm…" began Fleur.

"I am, after all, a woman," Wendy proclaimed the fact as if it were a significant achievement rather than biological chance or the providence of God.

"I think we're just here to sing, not speak," Fleur said.

"Sometimes the question of whether to speak is not really a choice. Sometimes we are compelled to speak. Isn't that right Scott?"

I didn't say anything. (I already knew better). Wendy carried on anyway.

"Let me have the microphone. I'll empathise with them. I'll explain that I feel their pain. After all, I was once an avowed lesbian owing to the inherent brutality of man. I could then say that not all men are horrible, point to Scott and segue into the opening lines of 'Lean on Me'."

Fleur, I think, was lost for words. She glanced at me for help but unfortunately, I'm ashamed to say, there was none that I was prepared to give.

"I think we better just sing, like we were asked to, and leave the speeches to those who have been booked to speak."

"As you wish. I just think it's important to make a statement against domestic abuse wherever possible. Come Scott."

Wendy wheeled on her heel and strode away, without looking back, into the crowd of assorted charitably minded souls, gathered to support the fundraising efforts of a charity raising awareness of domestic abuse. The Funk Soul Family were in a (musically) sombre mood that night having been volunteered (by Fleur) to appear free of charge. (What a girl). It was my first gig. Wendy had insisted I join the performance even though I didn't really know the songs and I was the only one without an official Funk Soul Family t-shirt.

But I agreed because Wendy compelled me to agree and also because I thought I might get to spend some time with Fleur. Her pleasant face had much been in my thoughts.

"This really is a very worthy cause," I said to Fleur as soon as Wendy was out of earshot.

Girls usually tend to roll their eyes at the banality of my conversational openers. ("Terrible weather we're having. I see the Bank of England have frozen interest rates again"). But not Fleur. (She was either a fan of banality or didn't find me banal). She agreed heartily with me and, again, stared me right in the eye.

"It is. It really is. It's quite humbling to think what some women have endured right under our noses."

"And some men," I offered tentatively.

"Scott, here now," Wendy bellowed through the crowd.

"Yes, some men," Fleur said as I tottered off with a smile and a whimper.

Chapter 4

"Feminism"

Project #7(ish) – Petra the Pessimist (unsuccessful and quite short)

In the third year of university I met Petra the Pessimist. (That was a suffix I gave her, rather than one she gave herself obviously). Petra was like a ray of sunshine to no-one, not even herself. The glass wasn't half empty; the glass was a pointless article of indifference wafting listlessly in the redundant nothingness of the universe. (I've paraphrased for her). Her dominant facial feature was a down-turned mouth. Her dominant personality characteristic was a down-turned attitude. She wasn't mean or degrading or particularly annoying, she was just glum.

She was in one of my seminars and I immediately gravitated towards her, on the basis that everyone else was gravitating away from her. (They had obviously met her). I sat at her elbow and engaged her in conversation.

"This new module is fascinating isn't it?"

"Is it? I don't think so," she said in a rather bored monotone.

"Well, maybe the subject itself isn't that interesting, but the tutor is really making the subject come alive, isn't she?"

"Not for me."

"Well, at least it's a beautiful day."

"Is it? I hadn't noticed."

The other students were tittering behind their hands, whether at my inept attempt at a chat up line or at the hopeless, downbeat, forlorn comments that came back at me. I ignored them and tried to smile at Petra as much as possible during the seminar. She didn't smile back, but she did occasionally turn her mournful eyes upon me, reminiscent of a sleepy, uninterested dog. It was all the encouragement I needed.

"I don't suppose you fancy a coffee?" I said as soon at the other students were out of earshot at the end of the seminar.

"I don't like coffee."

"Tea?"

"I don't like tea."

"A gin and tonic?"

"I don't like the smell of alcohol."

"Well how about we just go the pub and you pick something you might like."

I ensconced us in a nice little corner of the Student Union and placed a glass of tap water and a packet of pork scratchings before her (at her request you understand). She didn't say thank you.

"Well, this is nice," I offered.

"Is it? I don't like this place."

"The Union? How can you not like this place? The drinks are virtually free and you only have to wait a few minutes before some idiotic student does something entertaining, ridiculous or criminally insane…"

"Exactly."

We sat in silence for a few moments as I pondered my next move. This girl had Project written all over her, I just needed to think of a way to entice her, so I set myself to some hard thinking. She, on the other hand, smashed through an entire bag of pork scratchings in less than two minutes. Even the massive curly ones that are difficult to get into your mouth were despatched summarily. To look at her, you wouldn't think she was the kind of girl who would polish off fat based products in an instant. She was as thin as a rake with perfectly round spectacles on her down-turned face. Her hair was neatly combed into a tight, no-nonsense bun and her shoes were sensible and flat.

"They were nice," she said in a rather bored sounding voice, as soon as the last scratching had slipped down her gullet.

I almost did a double take, but I'm far too suave and experienced with girls of various personality disorders to be thrown by something so obviously out of character as that.

"You like the pork scratchings?"

"Yes."

"Would you like another pack?"

"If you're offering."

"I am offering."

"Then I'll have some."

"Why do you like pork scratchings so much?"

"Just do."

"You don't look the type."

"Looks can be deceiving," she said with nothing approaching mystery or coquettishness in her voice.

"Can they? Are you a deception?" said I, with as much flirt and subtext as I could squeeze into my vocal tone.

"Me?" she asked, perhaps of herself. "No. People think I'm miserable and I am."

"Why?"

"Why what?"

"Why are you miserable?"

As she formulated an answer I started to allocate Petra her Project Number (#7) and to work out a way in which I could alleviate her misery. It all fell quickly in to place; I would relentlessly compliment her, I would tell her how pretty she was, I would praise her every witty remark, I would buy her gifts, I would parade her around on my arm with pride, I would ravish her at every opportunity, I would inexorably build her self-confidence until she became a sunnier version of herself. I would degrade myself if that's what it took.

I'll turn that frown upside down, I said to myself without any hint of self-awareness.

"I don't know why I'm miserable. I just am."

"I'd like to help you."

"How?"

As she swirled the remaining bits of salt and fat from the bottom of the packet, I chose that moment to strike...

"I find you very attractive..." I began. I was looking at the floor under the pretence of embarrassment. I planned to glance up at her, through my long, expressive eyelashes, and look her straight in the eye. Never fails...

"Let me stop you there Scott." Petra put up her hand as I looked up through my long, expressive eyelashes that she was entirely ignoring. "Because I think I know where this is going. I have just told you that I'm miserable. You can see that I'm miserable. You can also see that I'm not very attractive..."

I started to protest but was cut off.

"...so in your simple little mind you've decided that all I need is some compliments, some attention and perhaps a good hard shag and I'll be a different person. You think that all I need is a shot in the arm and all will be right with the world. Isn't that right?"

I had to admit that it was.

"If you think the world is that simple Scott, you are really very, very thick."

And she got up and left.

Project #1 – Sal Pax (dead)

I never really did fancy Sally Paxton. It's not that she was unattractive, because she wasn't. She was quite pretty, albeit in quite a square jawed kind of way. And I didn't particularly mind the impetigo on her chin or the socks she had rolled around her ankles. I even found the electric shock hairdo fairly endearing. But I didn't fancy her. It's just that, in some small section of my mind perhaps filled with misogyny and my own superior moral discipline, I wanted to protect her. I wanted to make an honest woman of her.

I couldn't bear the things people said about her when she hadn't really done anything wrong. She'd just kissed a few boys, that's all. But, in my school, that made her a slut, even if it would have made an equivalent boy a stud.

"I'm what they call a feminist," I said to Dave (my best friend) once.

"You're an idiot," said Dave.

"You don't get many male feminists, because it's very difficult to free your mind of ingrained cultural prejudice – but I've managed it," I said.

"Don't look so smug," he said.

(I was looking smug, I'll admit. I was feeling ahead of my time. I was feeling like a visionary. I was very much the Christopher Columbus of adolescent sexual politics).

"And," Dave continued, "you're not a feminist, you're just frigid."

I just laughed at this typical example of male small mindedness. It sounded so old hat, like something my father might think but not say. I pitied him really, this Neanderthal Dave, he just couldn't see what I could see.

"In fact, you're more sexist than me," he said.

"How on earth…?"

"You think I'm sexist because I just want to have sex with girls," said Dave. "I'm only interested in one thing, tits…"

"That's two things."

"…so you think that makes me sexist. It doesn't; it makes me horny. And so I'll do anything I can to have sex with a girl; I'll lie, I'll cheat, I'll cry, anything. I have to be really on my game if

I'm going to get anything from a woman because they're clever, they've got morals, they know their own minds these girls. You've got to treat them like equals if you want to get anywhere."

A phrase about giving a man enough rope sprang to mind as he continued....

"You, on the other hand, you're a real sexist. Because you think they're defenceless, you think they can't look after themselves. You think they need help to get through life. Help from you – a man. Riding to the rescue on a big, sexist horse. You don't think anything of women, not really. They're not as strong, resourceful or as clever as you – and that makes you sexist."

"I'm just trying to help..." I objected to this diatribe of what (actually) sounded like logical and coherent thinking with perhaps even a hint of truth within it. I had, ever since I could remember, been predisposed to helping the female of the species – whether it be by opening doors or picking up dropped items or giving advice on how to carry the one in long multiplication. I felt Dave was deliberately misconstruing my attitude of helpfulness...

"Yes, you are, you're trying to help like a little boy who finds a bird in his garden with a broken wing. That bird won't survive without your help, that's how you think. Me, on the other hand, I know that women aren't little birds – they're lions – and if you want to shag a lion you've got to track it, overwhelm it and then hump it as if you're a bigger lion," said Dave, losing his way somewhat.

"Dave, what you have just said is abhorrent."

"I don't know what abhorrent means, but if it means "true" then I agree."

So when I eventually plucked up the courage to ask Sally Paxton to be my girlfriend, with a view to making an honest woman of her, I did so with a vague sense of guilt about my person.

Project #15 – Me (sounds vain)

"Are you OK?"

I was sitting on a bench, in a park near work, gazing into space and thinking about life, the universe and Sally Paxton, when Fleur walked past.

"Oh hi, yes, I'm fine." I said, turning the smile back on.

"I don't think I've ever seen you not smiling before. You even smile when you sing. Is everything alright?"

Fleur sat down next to me and I felt a surge of absolute contentment; like a feeling of "rightness." We were made to sit on benches together, we were made to buy crockery together, we were made to feed ducks together and make tea for each other...and I wanted to tell her that but I wondered if it might have been a little forward bearing in mind I'd only met her a couple of times.

"I'm fine."

Fleur looked at me; pleasantly.

"Did you enjoy the gig the other night? We weren't very good were we? The choir I mean. The sopranos were all over the place."

"I beg to differ. It was brilliant. We were brilliant. Very worthy."

"I get the feeling you never say anything bad about anything or anyone," she said, seemingly as a compliment.

"I do sometimes."

"I don't believe it."

"I do, honest. I have a friend called Dave who is a complete idiot. And my father is a bit of a plonker too."

"Don't hold back...!" she said with mock horror.

I smiled. "Ah, that feels good, to get all that anger off my chest."

Fleur looked at me, directly in the eye – again.

"You're sweet," she said.

"Thanks," I said.

Chapter 5

"Nosey"

Project #2 - Nicola the Nose (Successful)

Nicola was an inwardly beautiful girl. One of those quiet, intelligent, hardworking girls who sit near the front of class and never get into trouble. She was just a really nice person, although it took some considerable time to work this out as she was so painfully shy. In lieu of the difficult task of actually getting to know her, people just assumed she was nice because she obeyed her parents and did her homework. She hoovered up top exam marks at school and hoovered up domestic detritus at home to help her mum. She was never late and she never said anything nasty about anyone. She was the kind of girl that could easily go unnoticed through school. And even life.

But Nicola, for all that inner beauty, had one distinguishing outer feature that made her entirely noticeable. Her nose. It was huge. It was mighty. It was Romanesque. If she were a snowman you would need a competition winning parsnip to capture her likeness – no carrot would do.

It didn't matter that she was ridiculously nice. It didn't matter that she had lovely, luscious brown hair and almost reached her waist. It didn't matter that for all her obvious intelligence she said "nuffink" instead of "nothing." The nose conquered all.

Nicola was in love with Dave – the thick set, thick witted Adonis of sixth form. She adored him. She worshipped him. One night, during our first year of sixth form, in the local pub that served under-age drinkers without qualm or question, Nicola plucked up the courage – a courage that had been building for over six years – to say hello to Dave.

I was sitting at a corner table, waiting for Dave to bring me my drink. Dave, quite possibly the best looking kid in school, who would have been the captain of the school rugby team had we had one, the kid with all the designer labels and oodles of dispensable income, happened to be my best mate. We were quite an unlikely pairing; an alpha male and one somewhat further down the alphabet but our relationship was a win-win situation for us both. I was friends with him in the hope that some disorientated girls might throw themselves at him and hit me instead. He was friends with me because he had access to an infinite supply of free chips.

I could see Nicola steeling herself – visibly building herself for the grand moment. She was dressed in a rather unfetching black smock, accessorised by a sweeping green scarf cum waistcoat. She sipped slowly on a rum and coke. Her avalanche of hair was pinned in such a way as to hold her locks behind her ears and somehow accentuate the size of her behemoth of a nose.

She had barely taken her eyes off Dave all night. He was wearing a tight white t-shirt to accentuate his bicep muscles and tight blue jeans to emphasise his brain. Even I, a firm heterosexual, thought he looked good.

When Dave headed to the bar for another round of drinks, Nicola seized her chance.

As Dave stood at the bar, legs wide apart (dominating his space), Nicola quietly slid into the miniscule space next to him. Her heart must have been beating furiously. Her mouth must have been dry. Her nerves must have been frayed. But, she downed the last of her rum and coke and went for it.

"Hello Dave."

Dave heard his name, turned, smiled and then said something...from my vantage point I could see his lips move but couldn't make out the actual words.

Now, the thing about Dave is that he was (and is) as thick as he was (and isn't so much now) good looking. But he wasn't conventionally thick. Dave was "delusionally" thick in that whilst he realised he didn't have the academic smarts, he thought all his intelligence had been concentrated into one inescapably clever characteristic – wit.

Unfortunately, it hadn't.

This led into Dave trying to be funny. All of the time. Dave was under the mistaken impression that he was hilarious. He thought he was quick-witted. He thought he was a beacon of mirth. A side-splitting comic genius.

Most of the nicknames I had in my youth, "Chip Shop Scott," the "Tango Tosser," and indeed the inescapable "Second Hand Scott" all came mainly from Dave. Yes, he was my best friend all the way through school, (and yes he had punched Alex Simpson for me once after he'd trampled on my bag), but that was secondary to his role as a stand-up comedian. He would never ever pass up the chance to tell a joke or to deliver a witty put down; even if the consequences were horrendous.

So when Nicola said "Hello Dave," in a sweet little tremulous voice at the bar, he searched within his inner comedy catalogue and responded with…(as he told me later):

"Hello Bergerac."

Nicola fled from the scene with tears in her eyes and a reduced sense of worth in her soul. Dave brought the beers back to our table, chuckling to himself.

"Nicola Big Nose said hello to me at the bar and I said, "Hello Bergerac." It was hilarious."

"Was it?"

"Of course it was. I just said it. Like that. Just witty like that, no thinking or anything. I don't even know who Bergerac is, I just knew it was funny."

"Hmm."

Dave was slightly miffed at my underwhelming response to his to his riotous repartee.

"What's wrong with you? You usually find stuff like that really funny."

"Everyone's looking at me."

Dave looked around the pub. A few people were looking over in our direction but they were females too attractive to be taking any interest in the Charity Shop Chink.

"No-one's looking at you Scott. No-one ever looks at you."

"They are."

I had been hunched in the corner all night, trying to escape attention but being careful to watch and analyse and observe my fellow sixth formers. This was the first time I had been out since I had killed Sally Paxton just a few months before. I was afraid of the anger that would be directed my way, the derision, the contempt, the wrath. I had confined myself to my bedroom for a number of weeks; afraid of vigilante retribution. It hadn't come but still…when Dave did eventually persuade me to come out of hiding, it was with considerable trepidation.

"Scott, you're an idiot. No-one cares."

"You can't kill a fellow student and not expect some consequences."

"Scott, no-one even liked Sally Paxton. She was a right slag."

"In the newspaper they said she was a likeable and popular student."

"She was…to the men's hockey team." He paused for a moment to admire his own joke. "They loved her. No-one else cares. They have to say that stuff in the papers."

I looked around the room again. It was true that no-one was, at that moment, looking at me but that was evidence in itself. No-one *dared* look at me. How do you look into the eyes of a killer without flinching?

"If you want to forget Slaggy Paxton why don't you pop outside and have a bash with old Bergerac?"

"What?"

"Have a look…"

Dave indicated that I should look out of the window. Nicola was sitting on a wall outside the pub, sobbing her little heart out.

"She's vulnerable…" said Dave, raising an eyebrow.

"Do you think…?"

"Bergerac could do with a bit of cheering up, as do you, you miserable git. Get out there, say that her nose isn't that big and then grab her tits. She'll love it. If she doesn't, pretend it's some ancient Chinese tradition…"

I found myself outside, easing myself (sympathetically) into position next to Nicola. Dave was watching through the window, urging me on and laughing in equal measure. His parting words…"Make sure she doesn't poke you in the eye with her massive nose"… had been a real comfort.

"What do you want?" Nicola asked when she saw me through the tears.

"I just came to see if you were alright…"

She may have been nice, but she wasn't stupid and she saw through my opening line immediately.

"Is this why they call you Second Hand Scott, because you try to pick things up second hand – even girls?"

I put on a wounded expression which, for a wonder, actually worked – because Nicola was pathologically inclined to think the best of people.

"I'm sorry," she said. "That was rude."

(Rude but accurate, so I changed tack).

"Dave told me what he said. I'm sorry about that. He's a bit of a knob."

"I really like him."

"I know you do. But you're too good for him."

"Ha! You're such a liar. He's beautiful."

"Yes, he is on the outside, I'll grant you that. But he's also really thick on the inside, you've got to admit that."

Nicola smiled a little smile and glanced at me out of the corner of her eye.

"I'm not even certain he can tie his own shoelaces," I said. (An old classic).

That got a titter.

Nicola turned to look at me. I could see Dave through the window, miming a kiss with an imaginary girl, urging me on. He then mimed the action of groping a pair of breasts so I decided to stop looking at him.

"He can never open a door properly. He pulls when he should push and vice versa. He can walk faster than he can read, that's his problem."

Nicola laughed at that and I felt the moment was ripe for a compliment.

"You're really pretty when you smile." (Another old classic).

"Do you think so?" said a blushing Nicola.

"I do. I think you're lovely."

"Scott, you're really silly."

"I am silly. I know that. Silly old Second Hand Scott. But I know a nice girl when I see one. And you're a nice girl."

And then I kissed her. I'm not sure how I did it. I'm not really sure how you get from the wanting-to-kiss-a-girl stage to the actual kissing-a-girl stage – there is no science to it. I'm not sure how I negotiated the nose either; I think it slid into a space beside my ear.

But I kissed her gently and sweetly, or something that I thought resembled gently and sweetly. And she kissed me back. It was lovely.

After a moment or two we disengaged and I imagined, in the split second that we looked into each other's eyes, that we would become an "Item" and be childhood sweethearts and then get married and have big nosed oriental looking children and all would be perfect and lovely and idyllic. But Nicola just stroked my cheek, said "Thank you Scott, that really helped," and then headed back inside to get another rum and coke.

She left me on the steps, remembering her taste and wondering where she had gone. But I felt good. After what had happened with Sally Paxton, it was nice to help someone. It took the edge off a little bit. I liked it.

Nicola, retrospectively, became Project number 2.

Project #1 – Sally (dodo)

Sally Paxton was a frizzy haired sort of girl. I'm not entirely sure what a split end is, but she looked like she might have had a few; reminiscent of Einstein in his pomp. She tried to describe it as natural curl but she convinced no-one. She had broad shoulders and spots in one corner of her chin that drew the eye. She always carried a Walkman and she wore leg warmers almost all the year round.

But despite all that, she was quite attractive.

Such is the inequality of life, Sally Paxton had a "reputation" all the way through school. By the age of eleven most of the boys in school claimed to have kissed her. By the age of fourteen most of the boys in school claimed to have slept with her. By the age of fifteen, two different boys claimed (in the same week) that they had impregnated her. I have no doubt that most of these claims were false, as did everyone else I imagine, but it didn't really matter, smoke and fire conveniently merged, and the received wisdom was that Sally Paxton was "easy" and that she would do literally anything, anywhere, anytime to anyone.

Dave was one of the worst.

"Old Shaggy Paxton was round at my house last night, throwing stones at my bedroom window, gagging for it," he boasted one Thursday break time.

"No she wasn't. No-one throws stones at windows except in the movies."

64

Dave is the only person in the world whom I would actively agitate. It just came naturally. Everyone kicks down I suppose.

"She was. Nearly put a hole in one of them because she was so desperate for it."

I tried to ignore him, particularly as I knew his house to be double glazed.

"Aren't you going to ask me what happened?" he said, rather put out.

"No."

"Well, I'll tell you anyway. I put my head out of the window and I shouted, "get lost, I don't sleep with slags on a Wednesday night…you'll have to wait for the weekend."

I had a look at my student planner and could feel his irritation as I did.

"That's a joke Scott, I set the joke up to make you think that I was outraged at the thought of sleeping with a slag but really it was just because I have a schedule for when I sleep with slags. I only sleep with slags on a weekend, not Monday to Friday. Did you not get it?"

"I did get it. I just didn't find it funny."

That hurt Dave's ego a lot. Not funny. As if.

"What's wrong with you? How could you not find that funny? You've got no sense of humour when it comes to old Shaggy P. Do you fancy her or something?"

"No, I don't fancy her at all. I just think people are mean to her. You only ever call her Shaggy Paxton. You think she's only interested in sex. You've pigeonholed her."

"She wanted me to pigeonhole her last night…"

I climbed on to my little soapbox and used my favourite Dave related phrase.

"Shut up Dave. You have no idea what she's like as a person. You don't know if her parents are nice or horrible or whether they're dead. You don't know if she's lonely or bored or whether she really is a tart. You just see her as a sex object."

"Any hole…"

"And don't say "any hole's a goal" because that's horrible and I will give you a dead leg."

"What's got into you?" he said.

"Nothing. Nothing's got into me. I just think that people shouldn't be condemned by one mistake. People can change can't they? People don't have to be defined by one moment of their lives, do they?"

"Is this about your mum…?"

"Of course it's not about my mum, why would it be about my mum? Why have you even mentioned her? It's about Sally Paxton – give her a break."

Dave looked at me, weighing me up, analysing me, considering the words of his oldest friend, processing them in that recess behind his good looks. And then completely missed the point.

"You do fancy her don't you?"

Project #15 – Wendy the Worst (definitely)

"I have heard disturbing rumours," said Wendy as she paced the room.

I was sitting on a chair; a single, straight backed chair in the middle of Wendy's bedroom. It had been deliberately moved away from the dressing table into the middle of the room, allowing Wendy to walk all the way around me, much like a gestapo officer during an interrogation.

As soon as I had arrived that evening, I had realised that something was amiss.

My usual routine was to ring the doorbell and wait for a number of seconds, if not minutes. After a sufficient period of time, designed to make me think that Wendy was doing anything other than just waiting for me to arrive, I would hear the curt command "Come."

Within a minute of entering the house I would usually be naked. She would leap upon me with terrific ferocity and strip me bare, like a horny piranha. A few short moments of well-directed sexual shenanigans would follow, "put your hand there," "squeeze this," "wiggle that about now," until she was satisfied. (Although she said "satisfied" was the wrong word. It was too strong to describe my sexual skills). Then she would cradle my head upon her bosom and smoke a cigarette.

After I had made her a cup of tea, I would then fill her in on the minute detail of my day – most of which she already knew because she used every conceivable opportunity to come onto my floor at work and mark her territory. (By speaking to me and about me in a very loud voice - as opposed to rubbing herself up against furniture).

But that evening had been different. She opened the door before I had even rung the bell and escorted me upstairs without saying a word. I had been there for a full five minutes before she spoke and my clothes were entirely intact – I had never felt so naked.

"I have heard disturbing rumours," she said again.

"Have you?" I asked.

"Very disturbing."

She tried to bore her gaze into my head but I just smiled back until she gave up.

"One of my sources tells that you were seen sitting on a bench the other day."

Oh dear. (Sources? I bet it was one of the old dears from the Work Choir – trying to curry favour).

"And you were not alone. You were with Fleur."

Oh dear, oh dear.

"And you were not smiling."

Oh dear, oh dear, oh dear.

"Confess."

I did. I had to. I knew there was nothing I could keep from her. The dirty truth had to come out...

"Fleur sat next to me. On the bench," I said.

"Go on."

"And then I went back to work."

"Tell me more."

"There is no more," I assured her.

Wendy put her fingers into the shape of a steeple and gazed at me across her fingers. I wondered if she was going to break up with me...

"Describe Fleur to me."

"Describe her?"

"Yes, tell me what she was wearing, how she smelt, whether you noticed a flush on her throat, the way she crossed her legs, everything."

"Erm, she was wearing a dress and she smelt quite nice."

"No, no, no, Scott. If you're going to get out of this room alive you're going to have to give me every available detail...a vivid and sensuous reconstruction..."

Chapter 6

"Slapping"

Project #3 - Sonya the Slapper (Successful)

Helping Nicola gave me quite a nice warm feeling inside. She had been an emotional wreck; a broken spirit, a bruised soul - after Dave had dismissed her with his talk of Bergerac. (He still doesn't know who Cyrano de Bergerac is). But I, amiable, affable, helpful person that I am, had managed to lift her spirits. I'd cheered her, restored her confidence. I had *helped her*. After managing to kill Sally Paxton within only a few weeks of being her boyfriend, this was a welcome change. It felt good. In fact, it felt brilliant.

But I wasn't quite able to allocate a Project Number to Nicola because I didn't, at that point, realise I was a Project Driven Individual. No, it was Sonya who set me on that path.

Dave had persuaded me to hit the town with him, a few weeks after my little smooch with Nicola. That initial feeling of contentment, in seeing Nicola walk away from me with a smile on her face and a spring in her step, had been tempered slightly by the fear that my fellow students (many of whom had witnessed my passionate encounter with Nicola on the wall outside the Pig and Whistle) would be disgusted by my callous behaviour, so close to the untimely death of Sally Paxton.

"Did you see what he did?"

I stayed in my room for a week or so and waited for the tidal wave of accusation to hit me via emails, texts messages or bricks through my window. Said tidal wave never came and Dave eventually persuaded me to go out with him for a few drinks.

"Honestly mate," he said, "everyone has forgotten about her already. Come out and see for yourself."

So I did; albeit in an unconvinced and suspicious mindset.

But it turned out he was right.

"Hey Chinese Scott is here! Chinky Logan, good to see you! Where have you been? Not studying I hope…"

"Second Hand Scott, I'd heard you'd gone on a ballroom dancing tour…"

These were typical of the various drunken exclamations throughout the evening as various fellow sixth Formers clutched me to their bosoms. Not a single mention of Sally Paxton all night. I kept thinking about her though. Until I saw Sonya Peel.

Dave was leaning heavily on me, consuming his seventh pint of lager. I was nursing my first rum and coke because I wanted to keep my wits about me in the event of a vigilante attack upon my person and also because I get drunk very, very quickly.

"That's because you're Chinese. The Chinese are famous for getting drunk quickly. It's genetic. That's how karaoke got invented, drunk Chinese people."

"But I'm not Chinese. I'm English."

"So your mum says…"

I had had this conversation with Dave about a hundred times, usually after he had watched me rush to the toilet in a vomit-fuelled panic post impulsive Sambuca or spiked ginger beer. Getting drunk usually involved for me an immediate spinning sensation, followed by waves of nausea. A few moments later I would projectile vomit somewhere or other. Dave loved to see this, so he made every effort to get me drunk every time we went out.

"Seen anyone?" Dave squelched into my ear as he tried to undress every single woman in the club with a glance.

"No. As usual."

"Nicola Big Nose is here if you're desperate, I saw her upstairs on the dance floor. Big wide space around her as people tried to avoid her beak."

"She's with her boyfriend," I said with just a hint of bitterness in my voice. I couldn't believe it when I heard that Nicola had somehow bagged herself a boyfriend just a few short days after we'd had a game of tonsil tennis. George Williams – one of the most boring people in sixth form. It was an insult to my suitability as a potential life-partner that I was trying desperately not to take to heart.

"Yeah, but have you seen the state of him? He's tiny. Even you're better looking than him."

I was about to thank Dave for the backhanded compliment when our attention was drawn by a strikingly blonde girl slapping a man repeatedly around the head. This kind of event on a student night out was absolute gold dust and everyone in the vicinity was watching with keen interest. She was really going for him too; slap, slap, slap. Just pounding him with a flat hand around the temple area. The fact that he was laughing made it all the more entertaining for us and infuriating for her. After a while she stopped hitting him, they exchanged words and he left, quickly followed by another strikingly blonde girl who had been hiding behind a large padded chair.

A few moments after that, the original strikingly blonde girl was at the bar, drowning her sorrows. A few jiffies after that, I was standing next to her with my best sympathetic (yet smiling) face on – having received an encouraging push in the small of the back from Dave.

"Hi, I'm Scott."

"Sonya."

"That's a nice name."

She stared at me with utter, utter derision, such was the quality of my opening gambit.

"I've just seen my boyfriend kissing another girl in full view of everyone and then laugh about it when I caught him and you come across and say "that's a nice name.""

She shook her head with absolute contempt and took a long slug of her drink.

"Sonya...Sonya..." I rolled the name across my tongue a couple of times, soldering on with my seduction. "I wonder if that's Scandinavian in origin..."

"If you've seen me and thought you could come over here and get an easy shag because I'm vulnerable why don't you just say it? Get it out in the open?"

Tricky ground here...

"Perhaps it's Russian originally. Sonya. There was a novel published in 1917 that..."

"If I buy you a drink, will you stop talking?"

I nodded my affirmation and she bought me a whisky on the rocks (without asking what I wanted). She got one too.

"Down it?" she asked as she threw hers down her throat.

Honour compelled me to follow suit...

Some indeterminable time later I found myself lying naked on a bed while Sonya sat astride me doing things that I found initially quite pleasant. But then Sonya started to cry – without stopping what she was doing to my appendage – which made me feel slightly uncomfortable. As she increased her vigorous rocking about my person, she started to part-chant and part-cry: "I hate men, I hate men, I hate men."

Some women, for some reason, perpetuate the stereotype that the act of sexual union for a man is an entirely physical act. The implication being that men do not care about the emotional connection underpinning the intercourse. This is, of course, not true – particularly when you have a strikingly beautiful blonde woman riding you for all your worth whilst crying and denouncing mankind. It does have an effect.

"Can I slap you?" asked Sonya via the garbled words of the emotional and sexually active inebriate – as she slapped me forcefully in the face.

"Sorry I didn't catch that?" I said as she lashed out again.

"I just need to slap you," she mumbled again as she slapped me.

"I'm really struggling to hear," I said, when I should have been saying, "Why on earth are you slapping me?"

In fact, I never did actually make out what she was trying to say. It was only when I pieced together the underlying intent of her slapping action that I was able to reconstruct that conversation.

By the time she was finished with me my cheeks were as red as my manhood and my jaw ached as much as my inner thighs.

Sonya eventually wore herself out and crumpled onto the bed in fits of emotion. I tried to place a comforting hand on her shoulder but she said "don't" and so I didn't – just in case she started to slap me again.

Once she had finished crying, Sonya helped me into my clothes and showed me to the door. She was quite polite and solicitous.

"I'm sorry about that Scott. I guess I just wanted to hurt a man and you were the closest thing I could find."

"It's OK," I said, wary of another blow; physical or verbal.

"It really helped though. I feel much better. Thank you."

"You're welcome."

"Maybe you should do this kind of thing professionally. Help girls who just need someone to be there."

"As a punching bag?"

"A punching bag. A penis. A person. Whatever they need. That could be you."

As she shut the door in my face, an idea was born.

Project #1 – Sally Paxton (extinct)

Dave always used to have a sleep in the first period of school on a Monday morning. He would lock his thick arms together and rest his heavy noggin on them with a view to catching forty winks. The teacher of that lesson would then say (but only making that mistake once): "David, how can you possibly be so tired first thing on a Monday morning?"

"Because I didn't get an ounce of sleep that's why. The walls in our house are really thin and my parents were shagging into the early hours last night."

"Thank you David, that's enough…"

"Every Sunday night they are at it, regular as clockwork….bang, bang, bang….slap and tickle…going at it like rabbits."

"Yes David, I think we've heard…."

"Say what you want about my parents but they have got stamina. I'm surprised my dad's knob hasn't fallen off…"

"David, out!"

My uncontrollable giggling would almost get me thrown out too. The whole class found it hilarious. All except Sally P. She would laugh at anything usually, particularly anything lewd. But not this.

Other students have told me similar stories; unwholesome noises creeping under doors; sexy shenanigans seeping down the hallways, "turn over Mildred, I'm not finished with you yet."

I didn't have any of that.

I can't remember a single night when my slumber was disturbed. The only noise I ever heard coming out of my parent's bedroom was silence, which is an oxymoron. (Coincidentally, that was one of the nicknames Dave tried to stick me with in secondary school when I developed a small case of acne. Fortunately, it didn't quite catch the public imagination…mainly because it didn't make much sense). I never saw my parents kiss, cuddle or canoodle. They barely looked at each other now that I think of it. Even when they were squeezed together behind the counter at the shop, they somehow managed not to invade the personal space of the other.

There was one night though, when my sleep was disturbed.

I was very young, five or six perhaps, and I would have been sleeping quietly in my hand-me-down bed. I seem to remember the bed frame was in the shape of a car but with one the wheel arches broken off. At some point in the night, I awoke to find myself being carried downstairs. I was slumped in my father's arms, as close to him as I had been before or since. I must have dropped off again and the next thing I knew I was waking up in a little bed in a little room in what I found out was the house next door to our shop – the hairdressers.

I barely remember anything else about the morning. (I find the fact that I can't remember the details of this occasion whilst at the same time distinctly remembering that I should remember it most disturbing). What was the name of the couple who ran that coiffures? No idea. Did they give me breakfast? Can't recall. What did I do for clothes? Not the foggiest.

All I remember is my mum coming to take me home at some time during the afternoon. She looked tired.

No more was ever said about it.

Much like the day after Sally Paxton died. In the few short weeks of our relationship, my mum would often ask about Sally when my father was out of the room. I was grateful that she was interested.

But the day after Sally P was declared dead and forevermore, she was never mentioned again.

Project #15 – Wendy the Worst (getting worser – which should be a word because it's accurate)

"Hello darling," said Wendy, quite loudly, as she appeared behind me at my desk. Everyone on the floor turned to see, intrigued by the use of the word "darling" in the professional environment. Those who lingered over their glance were treated to the sight of Wendy grabbing my shoulders in what appeared to be an attempt at affectionate massage.

"You're tense," she said as she ground her thumbs into my spine.

(Of course I was tense; I was being assaulted in my workplace via maniacal massage).

"You need to relax. You're with me now."

That took me back to the first night we spent together.

After Wendy had dragged me away from the Funk Soul Family, she had bundled me into a taxi like some kidnap victim and had bid the driver to make haste to her house, for it was a "case of sexual emergency." The taxi driver just rolled his eyes.

As the meter ticked over Wendy explored my body with vigorous slaps and pats.

"Firm inner thigh."

"Sufficiently defined pectorals."

"Slight paunch around the middle."

"A protruding earlobe."

I felt like a horse, and I told her so in tremulous tones.

"We shall find out if you are like a horse in a just a few moments. Driver, quicker please!"

Wendy continued to grind into my shoulders as I tried to gloss over the stern physical examination she had given me that first night. (Now, I'm a fan of vigorous love making. To be frank, I'll take any lovemaking I can get. But a night spent with Wendy was altogether different. It was like Greco-Roman wrestling but with no option to surrender).

The next morning, I made it home and immediately booked an appointment with a physio. But I had to cancel it because Wendy wanted to go for a coffee and I had quickly discovered that Wendy always got what she wanted.

"Have lunch with me," said Wendy as she started hand chopping my neck.

I was about to make up some excuse (training session, seminar, Ramadan) when the hand chopping abruptly stopped. I waited for the pain to subside before raising my head...and there she was. Fleur. Walking down the corridor with a file of papers in her hand.

"I didn't know Fleur worked here," I said.

"Oh yes, she works here. Look like you're enjoying yourself," Wendy said as she began work on my upper body once more. "Do some moaning..."

I tried to smile as Fleur approached. She was wearing business clothes and looked...well, really quite pleasant and approachable once more. The kind of girl who would actually hold the lift for you, rather than pretending she was trying to hold it whilst secretly pressing the "door close" button.

She couldn't help but notice Wendy as she karate chopped my clavicles. She couldn't help but notice me; the person with whom she had shared a tremulously affectionate moment on a bench just a few days before. But she didn't even break stride.

"Morning lovebirds," she said with a smile not at all laced with regret or longing for yours truly.

Damn.

Wendy and I watched her go.

"What a cow," Wendy said.

Chapter 7

"Covering"

Project #4 – Carla the Cover Up (successful)

Carla was a lovely little dumpy girl from my sixth form. Dark haired, demure and delightful. She was in the same class as me for English and Politics and we often found ourselves sitting together. (I know now that teachers would often put the higher achieving students next to the ones who probably should have taken something vocational). Carla introduced me to the concept of relativity. Compared to Dave or my father, I was a veritable Albert Einstein. Compared to Carla however, I was a Village Idiot. She was sophisticated and cultured. She was fascinated by my "Ballroom Dancing Career." That is what she called it, my "Ballroom Dancing Career" although it wasn't really worthy of the capital letters. Carla was like that though, very good at assigning importance to anything, just in the way that she pronounced it.

In our Politics class she would often talk of the Oppression of the Masses or the Subjugation of the Working Class. In English she would regularly mention Gothic Post Modernism and Feminist Critique. (I may have got those mixed up – it could have been the Subjugation of the Gothic Feminists). In life too, she was At It. The Recklessness of Youth (any night club drinking game), the Anticipation of Failure (upcoming exams) and the Ballroom Dancing Career (my ballroom dancing career).

Her small head had a bobbing quality which gave her the impression of being interested in you. It just went up and down when you spoke to her; and you ended up thinking that she was hanging on your every word. She also spoke quite slowly, perhaps owing to all the capital letters she was trying to get into her speech.

"Did you win many competitions?" she'd ask, bobbily and slowly.

"A few."

"Did you have to travel up and down the country? Living The Dream?"

"No, I never really did that. Just entered the local competitions. I went to London once, but that was just for the day."

"I thought that was the life of a Ballroom Dancing Precocious Young Talent. Moving around, one competition to the next."

"It is for most people. There was a competition every weekend pretty much, all over the country. Regionals, nationals, European, even international if your parents are pushy enough – it's a massive scene."

"And yet you didn't go. Why not?"

"My mum never wanted me to."

(Odd that).

"Ah well, perhaps she was worried about you. All those young girls hanging around you. Adolescent Sexual Yearnings. Tell me about some of your partners."

Carla was lovely and we spent a fair bit of time together, discussing things that I didn't really understand…such was her level of cultural attainment. So much so that rumours started.

"Shagged her yet?" asked Dave as he tucked into a huge sandwich one lunchtime.

"No, we're just friends."

"So you haven't shagged her then?"

"I just said I hadn't."

"I didn't know if that meant you hadn't shagged or that you had but you were saying that you hadn't."

"It meant that I hadn't."

"You going to?"

"I don't know. It's not up to me, is it? I'm not a Neanderthal and I can't just club her round the head and drag her back to my cave."

"I bet they didn't have Neanderthals in China."

"I'm not Chinese."

"So your mum says…"

Carla was quite a classy girl. She enjoyed the theatre and art house films. She went to museums of her own volition and had even considered attending an opera or a ballet. I went with her to see a Shakespeare play one evening (or The Great Bard as Carla called him) and tried to stay with it as best I could. We sat in the theatre bar after witnessing nearly two hours of people shouting at each other in rhyming couplets and she cleared her throat.

"Scott, I've got something to ask you."

"If you want me to explain what just happened in the play I have no idea. Something about fairies I think…"

"It's not about the play."

I gurned at my foolishness. Of course she knew what the play was about. I was probably the only one in the theatre who didn't, although there had been a man who'd fallen asleep in the first act and slept through the interval too.

"It's about Us."

"I didn't realise there was an Us," I said, as a sense of impending doom descended upon me.

Carla was nervous, very nervous. It seemed to me that she was planning to break up with me, even though we weren't an item. I hadn't got much experience of being dumped at that stage (that was to come later) but I could intuit the signs. My new found acquaintance, Sod's Law, was just winding back his leg and getting ready to kick me in the balls.

"Well, that's just it…"

"Is it because I'm not clever enough for you?" (I thought I'd get in there early).

"What do you mean?"

"Is it because I smile too much?"

"I don't know what you're talking about."

"You see, even my questions aren't intelligent enough to be understood."

"Scott, what are…?"

"Is it because of Sally Paxton?"

"Who's Sally Paxton?"

"Sally Paxton. Remember?"

A light dawned in her eyes. "Oh her…? Sally? Why would it be about her? What's she got to do with it?"

She was obviously just being kind…

"I just thought I'd done something wrong," I said.

"Wrong? What could you have done wrong? Scott, you're a…"

…Lovely guy but I think it's time we stopped seeing quite so much of each other…

"…lovely, kind, understanding sort of guy and I wanted to ask you if you would be my boyfriend. If you Understand Me?"

Despite the fact that Dave was constantly doubting my true parentage, in that moment, I was quite convinced that my father was indeed my real father because I did what he always does in moments of stress, high jinks, elation, depression, good news, bad news, the apocalypse. I blinked. A lot.

"Are you OK?" Carla was starting to get quite concerned as I blinked profusely in her direction. "You're not saying anything."

"I don't know what to say."

"I know. I appreciate that I'm asking A Lot."

A lot?

She took my hand and gazed into my eyes (as I continued to blink) with a look of profound meaning in hers (that I missed entirely). She then delivered an important speech; the import of which I completely failed to comprehend.

"You know me, don't you? You know Who I Am. Who I Really Am. And you know that one day I'm going to be Who I Really Am but I can't be who I am at the moment because...well, because of everything: my parents, friends, college, society – the Scrutiny of Suspicion. But you know Who I Am. And I think you know that I need to explore myself, to build confidence in Who I Am. And if I have you, you'll be able to help me, won't you? Like a Shield. A Protector. An Incubator of Self Awareness and Self Confidence. You will shield me from the eyes of the world and I will be able to grow and flourish and Find Myself. Am I making sense?"

Not a jot, but I kept nodding throughout. *She wants me to be her boyfriend! Woo hoo!*

"Do we understand each other?"

"Absolutely." I had no hesitation in lying to her.

"So you'll do it? You'll be my boyfriend?"

"Without a doubt."

"Scott, you're amazing."

"So they tell me."

"You don't mind being Second Hand Scott...for me?"

"Not at all," said I, answering a question that I didn't understand, in the midst of a conversation that I didn't comprehend with a girl that I totally failed to fathom.

With that, she held my hand to her cheek and sobbed a little and I realised that this would probably be the girl that I would marry. If she was this grateful that I'd agreed to go out with her, just imagine what she'd be like when I unleashed my sexy moves on her or even brandished an engagement ring. I was set for life.

Now of course, on reflection, I realise I missed a bit of subtext there as she gazed into my eyes with Intense Profundity. But I promise you, that conversation was the only hint she ever gave me that she was a lesbian. Until she left me for a receptionist at the local sports centre, which eventually cleared it up.

"I honestly thought you knew," she said.

"I can't believe you didn't know," said Dave as he tucked into a plate of chips and gravy, whilst leaning against the counter in Fry Days.

I really didn't want to speak about this, not in the shop anyway. Mr Townsend, a regular, was sitting on one of the benches pretending to read the local free newspaper as he waited for his standing order – cod, chips and curry sauce. But I knew he was listening. My father was there too, frying. I wasn't even sure he knew what a lesbian was but he was definitely listening. I could tell from the rate of blinks.

"You can spot a lesbian from a mile away. I can anyway," Dave boasted. "They call it a "gaydar" and I've got it."

I just refused to respond. But he carried on...

"Firstly, they wear dungarees. Secondly, they're butch. Thirdly, they have short hair. Fourthly, they like Kylie Minogue. Oh no, hang on, that's gay men. And also, they drink a lot. Pints of beer usually."

"Well, Carla wasn't anything like that, as you well know."

Honestly, it was true. She never gave any hint of being interested in the opposite sex. None. (She did ask a few questions about my ballroom dancing partners but I thought that was more to do with the dance than the dancer). I mean, what's the point in being gay if no-one can tell?

"Well, she must have given you some clue," said Dave as he applied yet more salt to his chips, making a concurrent deposit on a robust paunch and heart disease. "What did you do when you were together?"

"Nothing, we just had intelligent conversations…"

"Well, that's a giveaway for a start," said Mr Townsend, giving up all pretence of reading about a proposed new by-pass. "Women who talk are generally those that talk, if you get me."

"No-one gets you Mr Townsend because that doesn't make any sense," I said, feeling at liberty to be rude to Mr Townsend because he only ever bought cod, chips and curry sauce.

"I get him," said Dave. "I know exactly what he means. What else did you do?"

"We just held hands and went for walks and went to the theatre."

"Unbelievable," exclaimed Dave, spitting a segment of chip on to the counter. My father wiped it up without a moment's hesitation. "How much more evidence do you need? Nothing says "I am a raging lesbian" more than holding hands and going to the theatre. Isn't that right Mr Townsend?"

"He talks sense this lad. All the lesbians I've ever known, and I've known a lot let me tell you, have been just like that."

"You're not thinking librarians are you?" I asked.

"One and the same thing my lad."

"You're both talking nonsense. No offence Mr Townsend." I said, at a look from my father. 'The customer is always right' was his unspoken motto – even those who spend less than three pounds. (Three pounds! Hence why my mattress had springs coming out of it…)

"None taken."

"Your problem is Scott, let's face it, is that you didn't want to know that she was a lesbian. You deliberately ignored the signs…" Dave said.

"There were no signs!"

"…because you were in love with her."

Dave, unfortunately, had hit the nail right on the head. For all his thick-witted prejudice and talk of dungarees and short hair he had, on this occasion, a gift of rare insight. I had loved her. Madly loved her.

And he was probably right, I had ignored the signs. Not signs that she was homosexual – I maintain there were none – but signs that she didn't really dig me in the way that would expect a girl to dig someone after she had sobbed into the back of his hand.

I have no idea what she thought I was doing when I touched her bum or tried to kiss her or sat with my hand on her inner thigh (at the theatre). Method acting perhaps. She never said anything and she never reciprocated. The only time she showed me any affection, beyond hand holding and using my shoulder as a head rest was when I met her parents.

"You do smile a lot don't you Scott?" said her father as I sat in his front room, smiling a lot.

"I do."

"Is there any reason for that?"

"Reason?" I asked.

"Yes, a reason."

He was a rather tall beanpole of a man and he hadn't smiled since I arrived. That wasn't quite so bad when Carla and her mum (an older, bobbier, dumpier version of Carla) had been in the room, but was quite unnerving when they weren't.

"A reason connected with my daughter perhaps?"

"I am fond of her," I said, dredging up some polite Victorian conversation from somewhere.

"Yes, you made that very clear indeed."

As I had made my way to Carla's house for the first time earlier that evening, I had received a text from Carla which said: "Mum just came to speak to me about how I shouldn't be afraid to be myself. If you know what I mean. It was quite awkward and I'm not ready for that yet. Really need you to be convincing tonight."

OK, so I admit it, that text might have been a clue but I thought perhaps she had made a typing error – perhaps she meant convivial, charming or conversational instead of convincing. So I set out to be all those things.

Carla opened the door to me and immediately attached herself to my face. I have to say, it was tremendous. A thrill went through my body and I found myself reciprocating without thought. My left hand, totally unbidden by my conscious self, lodged itself on to Carla's right buttock. My other hand instinctively began searching for a breast, any breast, but Carla's body was lodged so hard against mine that there was no space so it ended up just flapping about in excitement. As first kisses go, this was spectacular. However, somewhere after the fourteenth revolution of my tongue around Carla's mouth I became conscious of being watched.

I opened an eye, multi-tasking as I continued to wiggle my lips around the lower part of Carla's face, and saw a collection of people standing in Carla's hallway, watching. I later found out that these were Carla's mother and father, her sister and her Aunty Dorian. Not one of them looked particularly impressed. I removed my hand from Carla's bottom. Deprived of support she gradually succumbed to gravity and slid down my body. As soon as her lips dislodged from mine, I was able to put in place my habitual smile. Carla's father obviously equated that smile with the doorstep ravaging of his daughter he had just witnessed.

That was the only time she ever kissed me.

Project #1 – Sally Paxton (expired)

A few years before I started going out with Sally Paxton, she caused quite a stir at school by nearly blowing it up.

I'm exaggerating of course; the school was in no real danger of blowing up. But the local paper ran a sensationalist headline anyway, suggesting that it was.

Sally had become quite friendly with one of the lab technicians in the science block. He showed her the master switch for the gas supply to the classrooms because she was interested in his band.

One lunchtime, Sally was discovered in one of the classrooms in the science block, holding a flaming Bunsen burner under her arm, trying to write something or other beginning with the letter L. Or perhaps it was a seven, who knows.

That was fairly alarming for Mr Long, the teacher who discovered her. As was the fact that Sally had opened all the gas valves in the room with a view to perhaps killing herself in a flaming fireball. The chances of that were fairly slim though as the valves let out very little gas and Sally had left a window open. As suicide attempts go, it was fairly inept. You can imagine the fuss it caused though...lots of overreacting teachers, lots of attention from the powers that be and lots of students bemoaning the fact that the school failed to ignite into a deathly inferno, thus denying them a day or two off school.

People eventually forgot about it though; anything can become normal if you wait long enough. The lab technician was sacked and may have been added to some register or other, Sally P started wearing long sleeve t-shirts and the science block was locked at lunchtimes.

I didn't forget though. When Sally eventually returned to school I made a point of saying hello to her but she just flicked a cigarette butt (unlit) into my face.

Project #15 – Wendy (getting worse)

The first time I met Fleur I fell in something approaching love with her, albeit liberally sprinkled with lust. When she said hello to me at the bar, I instantly found her non-descript beauty attractive. She became lodged in my brain; but it was a manageable obsession (busy as I was with Wendy-related duties). Our chance meeting on the bench had wedged her further into my brain and my fleeting glance of her at work had titillated me. However, I was skilled at compartmentalising things - sexual attraction, emotional attachment, childhood memories, etc - so I was able to manage. But at my third Funk Soul Family rehearsal I fell completely in love with her - it was love at first touch - and it blew my carefully constructed compartments to smithereens. Just like that. I didn't believe that kind of thing could happen until that point - the old thunderbolt, Cupid's Arrow, the love at first...etc. But in the blink of an eye I was converted. And I can pinpoint the exact moment when it happened too; it was during the second chorus of "Lean on Me" when her bare upper arm touched the back of my hand.

Wendy encouraged me to stand next to Fleur during rehearsals - for a number of reasons. She wanted to show Fleur just how happy and in love we were, even though we weren't. It also gave Wendy an excuse to get near to Fleur and allowed Wendy to engage Fleur in conversation from time to time.

"Interesting article in the Guardian today about mental health..."

It also gave Wendy an opportunity to touch Fleur, under the guise of touching me. As we sang "Fields of Gold" by Sting, Wendy might reach out and stroke my bottom. As she did, she might accidentally caress Fleur's bottom. When Fleur glanced at her inquisitively, Wendy would hold up her naughty hands and shrug as if to say "what an easy mistake to make...being squeezed up as we are into a vocal and harmonic scrum in the interest of sonic solidity."

I tried not to notice. I smiled a bit, as you might expect.

There was a fair degree of jostling in that choral crowd, but Fleur was a bit like Jesus. Having been jostled by a throng, Jesus knew when a woman had touched the hem of his garment in faith. In the same way, Fleur could differentiate the hand of Wendy from any normal hand when it brushed, rubbed or otherwise fondled her in frustrated lust.

I don't know if she noticed the moment when the back of my hand touched her bare upper arm. I don't know if she felt the electric shock in the same way that I did. I was just moving my hand up towards my head to push a troublesome lock of hair away from my eyes when Fleur's body swayed towards me. Our skin touched, just for a moment. Our flesh became temporarily one. And it just felt…right.

The next note – a mid-range C – caught in my throat as my heart lurched to a place it hadn't lurched before.

Chapter 8

"Lying"

Project #8 – Gillian the Gerbil (successful)

My first job out of university was a fertile ground of crazy, needy ladies in need of the assistance of Second Hand Scott. The office had a nice mix of the embittered old lady and the young, dim-witted thrill seeker.

The first of these that I encountered was Gillian.

Gillian was a lady of generous proportions; of thigh, buttock and breast. She was fairly voluminous in the hair and cheek department too. Her voice was curiously high pitched (quite at odds with the depth of her bosom) and her laugh would not be out of place on a TV programme chronicling the various mating calls of the wild. All in all, she gave me the distinct impression of being descended from a long haired gerbil, or guinea pig, or chinchilla – it doesn't matter really, as long as it's a chubby rodent.

I shared my impression of Gillian with others in the office in the hope of becoming popular, "doesn't Gillian just remind you of a hamster," but there was very little uptake in the agreement stakes. One little shrew of a woman who happened to detest Gillian (owing to some altercation from an office Christmas party many years before) said that Gillian reminded her of a guinea pig but without the guinea. The office manager said, rather diplomatically, that she'd never envisaged any of her members of staff as being anything other than industrious beavers.

Gillian also had an unhealthy obsession with talking about herself. Which is not a particularly good trait at any time, but is most singularly bad when you happen to be very boring and squeaky. Most of Gillian's stories, anecdotes and tales tended to revolve around her going out on the town with her friend Carol, getting as drunk as possible and then resisting the advances of a host of sexy, rich, cultured yet sex-obsessed men – except occasionally when one lucky guy might be selected for a night of passion.

Now these kinds of stories are usually fairly interesting; illicit sex, gratuitous drunkenness, brushes with the long arm of the law. These stories are told all over the land on a Monday morning and are quite often lapped up by those desperate individuals wishing to live vicariously. (Those who spent the weekend in a garden centre or a soft play area). However, these stories fail to be in any way interesting when it is quite clear that the stories are untrue – lies even. Fabrications of falsehood.

Gillian was one of the most irritating of liars; one of those who would spin the most incredible yarns without sufficient depths of memory to be able to remember exactly what was said just a few moments before. And worse, she was one of those liars who would become mortally, irrevocably, irretrievably wounded if you happened to pick her up on one of the many contradictions that littered her narrative.

If you said, "…but I thought you just said he was an aeronautical engineer, not a milkman…" Gillian would write your name in her little book of vitriolic grudges and curse your name forevermore.

So regardless of the fact that everyone in the office knew full well that her crazy friend Carol was probably her mum and that "a wild night out" was code for "stayed in and watched a film" and that "this man was plying me with drinks all night, trying to get into my knickers," really meant "I haven't had a sniff in years but would really like to be sniffed quite vigorously" we all played along and nodded where appropriate.

It is, after all, quite an uncomfortable experience to catch someone in a lie – both for the catcher and the caught.

So when Gillian arrived at work one day wearing an engagement ring it took everyone by surprise.

Particularly me, as I had thought, up until that moment, that Gillian had the hots for me – judging by the kind of looks she gave me and the number of entirely pointless but ever so slightly flirty emails that she sent me. In ordinary circumstances I would have replied to every single one of those emails; sensing the possibility of a fresh Project. But I'd discounted her on two grounds: firstly, she didn't seem to need anything and secondly, that voice.

A few days into the surprise engagement I found myself speaking to her at the photocopier. This was one of her favourite tricks; to wait until I made my way to the photocopier and sidle in behind me to wait her turn and to ogle my tight bottom in the meantime.

I'd only gone to do a sheet but I heard her little squeaky noise behind me before I'd even managed to press the green button.

"Congratulations," I said.

"Oh, thank you," she squeaked demurely.

She wiggled her hand in front of my face.

"Wow, that's a big rock."

"I know," she squealed. "I said to Colin, well however much did it cost, and he said don't you worry your pretty little head about it and that I was worth every penny."

"Well, best get back then."

"He said to me that a man is supposed to spend a month's wages on an engagement ring but he just thought what the hell I'm going to spend two month's wages on it, so he did and you should have seen the manager's face in the shop when he pointed to this ring, the manager couldn't believe his eyes because he'd never sold such a big ring in all his years in the jewellery trade," she squawked as I tried to edge past her.

"You're a very lucky girl."

I was almost free when she put one of her breasts in my way.

"I said that to Colin, I said I'm a very lucky girl and he said no he was the lucky one, as lucky as a man who has just won the lottery."

"You're both lucky then."

I made a dodge for the open spaces of the corridor but the other breast caught me in a pincer movement.

"Some of the girls are going out tonight for a drink or two after work, to celebrate my engagement. Would you like to come?"

"Ah, well, I think I may have something else on tonight..."

She pouted and squeaked a little disconsolate squeak. "Oh Scott, please come. I'd like you to be there. It's a big moment for me."

I sighed. Why couldn't I ever say no to a girl? Even the ones with genuinely irritating vocal chords and / or a preponderance to lying.

"I'll be there."

And so I was, although no-one else was, apart from Gillian.

"Where is everyone?" I asked as I arrived at the designated celebratory watering hole as late as reasonably possible.

"Everyone's running late. Come and join me."

Gillian patted the seat beside her and so I had no choice but the deposit my tight little bottom there. The little alcove she had secreted herself into was fairly snug, meaning my tight little bottom was closer to her loose, expansive bottom than I would have liked. She had even bought me a drink, which she pressed into my hand immediately.

"Bottom's up," she said as she downed her drink. The peer pressure forced me to have a go at downing mine, although I could only manage half before coughing and spluttering a bit. Gillian hit my back gently, so gently that it somehow turned into a rub.

"Thanks for coming Scott. It's lovely to celebrate this happy and special day with someone that I consider also to be happy and special."

I smiled and did a little giggle as the drink went straight to my head. It seemed to be a particularly strong drink.

For the next hour, Gillian talked about how happy and special she was feeling and how happy and special Colin was and how happy and special the whole wedding was going to be and how happy and special I was. I kept looking at my watch and asking where the others were. Occasionally Gillian would say, "I'll have a look for them," but would reappear a few moments later shaking her head and holding two fresh drinks. She would push one into my hand and make sure her fingers brushed mine.

I started to get suspicious....

As my head began to swim I found myself tuning out of the "happy and special" monologue in order to concentrate on various aspects of Gillian's appearance. I'd never, for example, noticed the little spots on her cheek, mostly covered by make-up. I'd never noticed how grubby her finger nails were or the splodge of something sitting in the corner of her eye. (I'm guessing it was mascara). I found them slightly repulsive; these little imperfections. And as the room started to spin, I found them every more disgusting.

"Scott, I have something delicate I want to raise with you."

I tried to focus on Grubby Gerbil-like Gillian and found her staring at me intently. She didn't seem to be affected by the booze at all.

"When a woman is about to get married she comes to realise that one part of her life is over, she moves on to a new chapter, so to speak. She's about to commit herself to one man, and one man only for the rest of her life, to share his bed and only his bed for the rest of her days."

"Yes?"

"And so, even though I love Colin so much and know that he will make me happy and special for the rest of my life, because he says I'm one in a million and that he's won the jackpot of life, I have a strange desire...or maybe it isn't strange, you tell me."

"What is it?" (Idiot).

"To have one last fling. To have one last passionate encounter with a man who'll just treat me like a woman needs to be treated."

"Oh right." It was the only thing I could manage through the rising queasiness.

"And I want that man to be you Scott."

"Oh right." Still rising.

"Right here and now. Tonight. Have another drink."

"Oh right," I said once I had had another (ill-advised) drink. "Here?"

"Well, not here exactly, people might stare if we just got down to it right here in the bar. I was thinking we could go in the disabled toilet. I've used it before."

"I don't think I can."

"If you're worried about Colin, you needn't be, he'll never know, it will just be our little secret. A secret between our bodies."

"But I don't think I can."

"And don't you worry about getting caught. I know the Landlady here very well and she's very understanding."

"No, really, I don't think I can."

"Whatever is bothering you sweetheart, I can make you forget it all, I can make you feel happy and special," she whispered into my ear in what I can only imagine was an attempt at sultry seduction but which sounded to me like a guttural squeak.

And at that point, I was sick all over her shoes.

The next day Gillian was ashen faced and downbeat. She failed to respond to any of the "good mornings" offered her way and when someone suggested she partake of a restorative cup of tea, she started to sob quietly.

The atmosphere in the office was one part tense, one part intrigued and one part delighted. What could have caused Gobby Grubby Gerbil-like Gillian to be so quiet and moody? Why were her eyes so red? Why was her voice so raw? Why did she keep biting her fist?

I tried to keep out of her way, fearing that it was perhaps my projectile vomit that had caused this reaction. It cannot be easy for any woman, or any man for that matter, in the midst of urgent sexual advances to be interrupted mid-flow by a flow of quite another kind.

How on earth I got home and the pub got cleared up, I have no idea, (and I hope I never do). I had woken up that same morning in my bed, fully clothed, stinking of the congealed flecks of vomit that were spattered about my clothes. My head was throbbing and I could barely stand up without lights flashing in my eyes.

When popping to the stationery cupboard for a fresh consignment of staples I did notice that Gillian had a different pair of shoes on, and wondered if she might have been particularly attached to the ones I had blemished the night before. Could that be the cause of this obvious distress?

Perhaps her hangover was just worse than mine.

But around mid-morning, one of the post boys brought a package up from reception. He handed it to Gillian and said, "cheer up, might never happen," in quite an innocent attempt at joviality.

Gillian stood up immediately and threw the package straight at the post boy's head.

"But it has happened. It happened last night..." she shrieked, much like I imagine a Banshee to shriek.

"...my fiancée, my husband to be, in bed with another woman last night. We've only been engaged a few days but he said he wanted one last fling. So, tell me to cheer up again, if you dare..."

The post boy slinked away rubbing the side of his head as Gillian rounded on the office, brandishing her hand in the air.

"See? No ring. Satisfied? I know you've been prowling round, whispering in corners, trying to get some gossip – you horrible set of hyenas. Well here it is, the wedding is off. Satisfied now? Will this give you something to thrill your sad, little lives?"

Some people nodded as if to say, "yes, it has enlivened my sad little life, thanks", some looked away. Some openly laughed and hooted: "poor thing, it is terrible when your imaginary fiancée runs off with another woman."

Gillian ripped off her official work lanyard and headed for the door. Before exiting, she stopped, spun and addressed me in the loudest possible tones.

"Scott, come with me."

I pointed to myself. *Moi?*

"Yes, you, now, you gormless idiot. You know where."

The whole office looked at me. I smiled, shrugged and followed Gillian out of the door.

A few moments later, Gillian locked the door to the disabled toilet and took my clothes off. I did try to protest but she just kept stripping me bare.

"If you had been able to hold your drink and do your duty, I would never have gone round to Colin's house for some sex and would never have seen what I saw. You bloody, weak livered Chinese people. You owe me one."

So, for a few minutes, I gave her one of those things that I owed her.

A few minutes after that, Gillian left the building, all smiles and happiness and speciality.

And a few minutes after that, I was sacked.

And I never did work out whether Colin was actually real.

Project #1 – Sally Paxton (perished)

About a week after Sally and I became an "item" she appeared in my shop and asked for a cone of chips. My father gave her a cone of chips. She gave him 90 pence. (I mean, 90p in that day and age for a cone of chips – what a steal). She liberally applied salt and vinegar. And then she sat on the bench near the window and ate the chips.

I wasn't actually present for those actions; I'd been in the back sweeping up. But I have managed to reconstruct these events with reasonable confidence as Sally was sitting on the bench by the window with a cone of chips when I came through to the front of the shop. However, I should probably add that she wasn't alone. There was a man, an older man, sitting with her. An older, bedraggled, gnarled looking man.

Sally would take a chip, eat it, and then place her finger and thumb into the older man's mouth. He'd suck them, presumably getting a hit of salt and vinegar, with perhaps the hint of a potato. And perhaps a hit of something else too.

I didn't really know what to do when I saw her and I saw him. My father's eyebrows...well, they were expressive. I quickly slunk back to where I'd come from and swept the area that I'd just swept. I don't know if Sally saw me.

My mum asked me later that day: "...was that that girl you're friendly with I saw in the shop earlier?"

"Didn't see her," I said.

Project #15 – Me? (sounds pretentious)

My mobile phone rang with a number that I didn't recognise.

"Hello," I said.

"Good afternoon, is that the Professional Gooseberry? I'd like to book you…"

"Hello Dave," I said with a sigh.

"How did you know it was me?" he said with genuine incredulity.

"Because you're the only person in the world who remembers that I once was the Professional Gooseberry. Besides, that accent was horrendous. What even was it?"

"It was supposed to be Geordie."

"Well, it wasn't."

"Well, you can't be good at everything can you? I'll just stick to my strengths…giving orgasms to any woman who comes within three feet of my…"

"What's up Dave?" I interrupted before the inevitable vulgarity.

"Nothing, just ringing to organise our little monthly meet up. Piss up. Knees up. Large up. General all round shag-fest that occurs whenever Second Hand Scott and Big Dick Dave get together."

I groaned – audibly.

Ever since we had left school Dave had subjected me to regular visits; where he would drink, fart and snore his way through a long weekend. We didn't actually live all that far apart; he could easily have made it home in the evening. However, he always wanted to "make a weekend of it." And the weekend wouldn't be considered a success unless Dave woke up in a skip or got accused of sexual harassment. The frequency of these visits increased as the years went by as various wives left him and many of his other friends emigrated to Australia.

Dave laughed. "You better moan, mate. I'm going to fill you so full of alcohol you'll puke. That usually takes a pint. It's going to be great. See you at six. Laters."

He rung off and I banged my head against the nearest wall with as much force as reasonably possible.

On the bright side though, I thought, at least I'll get out of seeing Wendy for the weekend.

My phone rang again.

"Is this the professional gooseberry?"

A girl's voice this time. Dave must have another friend. I knew it was Dave because he was committed to his witty mantra: "the secret to comedy is repetition." Which is why he had retained his juvenile sense of humour since school.

"It is indeed."

"I was wondering if I could book you?"

"Of course, let me just get my diary."

I shuffled some papers on the desk in front of me – to play along. I had had no need of a diary at any point of the Professional Gooseberry endeavour. If I had had one, it would have been filled only with the everlasting emptiness of nothingness. Or, to put it another way, the Professional Gooseberry had earned me about £115 in total.

"When were you looking to book me?" I asked, using my professional sounding phone voice, perfected over many years of taking advance orders at the takeaway.

"This afternoon actually, if you're free?"

"As it happens I am, I've just had a cancellation."

"OK, I'll see you later then, at the corner of Queen's Street at 2pm. Looking forward to it."

The caller rang off; perplexing me. I had expected Dave to grab the phone at the last minute and shout something involving the words "gullible twat." Perhaps it was genuine. It was unlikely that Dave had more than one friend. And the voice did sound familiar. No, it couldn't be...

A couple of hours later I was waiting on a street corner, trying not to look like a prostitute or a gullible twat. I hadn't been given much information, other than a location and a time. I was tense; waiting for the tell-tale noise of Dave in full belly laugh mode..."you knobhead. I've come to kidnap you and sell your vital organs."

A car pulled up.

"Do you know it's illegal to loiter on street corners?"

It was Fleur, looking splendidly pleasant and slightly spotty as she leant out of her car window. (Please don't ask me what I'm doing...)

"Oh hi, how are you? Fancy seeing you here. I'm just waiting for someone."

"I know. Me."

"You?"

"Yes, I booked you for the afternoon." She looked delightfully pleased with herself; as if it were a grand jape.

"You? I thought the voice sounded familiar."

"I was using my phone voice to put you off. I didn't want you to think it was weird. Is it weird?"

"How did you even know that I'm the Professional Gooseberry?" I asked.

"I was looking you up on the internet. Does that sound weird too? It does doesn't it? You don't have to come if you don't want to."

To answer, I got in the car and said, "drive on."

She motored off. (Well, she stalled first and then carefully checked her mirrors and her blind spot before slowly pulling into the traffic).

"Where are we going?"

(Please say a hotel, or your place, or Lovers' Lane or a deserted alleyway or something...)

"I'm taking you to an RSPB nature reserve."

Damn.

"Why?"

"To look at birds of course. And also because we might have the chance to talk."

To talk...!

As we walked round the nature reserve, Fleur talked me through the various species on offer – as if she were my guide rather than me being her gooseberry.

"That's an avocet. And that's a bearded tit."

In the spirit of professionalism I did manage not to laugh whenever she mentioned tits, although it was an effort. I did my best to pretend to be interested as we wandered round but by the end of the afternoon I still couldn't tell the difference between a bittern and a marsh harrier. They all looked like indistinct blobs or flashings blurs.

We spent the whole afternoon together, walking close to each other, bumping arms, giggling occasionally. Well, almost all the afternoon. There were quite significant periods of time when we had to diverge from each other's company on the basis that I was wearing white plimsolls (the choice of the male gigolo) whilst Fleur was wearing Wellington boots that went above the knee. So, whilst I tried to negotiate the least muddy path through field and fen, Fleur crashed and sloshed her way through and over anything. Indeed, Fleur was so ridiculously well provisioned for a brush with nature that I was slightly miffed that she hadn't forewarned me. Besides the white plimsolls I was sporting some pale blue trousers and a salmon coloured scarf (amongst other things of course). I caused quite a stir at the nature reserve for my dashing style and obvious urban stupidity.

Fleur, on the other hand, fitted right in. She looked the very epitome of a bird watcher; oily coat, floppy hat, duck whistle and binoculars. She couldn't have looked more of a nerd if she tried, and I tell you, she had never looked more beautiful.

When we sat down on a log sometime in the mid-afternoon for a coffee miraculously produced from Fleur's rucksack, I was very tempted to ask, "how come you know so much about tits?" but restrained myself by reminded myself of that ancient Chinese proverb, "he that mentions tits, is one."

"It was my dad really. He loved the outdoors. Bird watching, hiking, climbing, anything really. He got me into it."

I knew the feeling of paternal inspiration, my father had similarly enthused me with his love of all things…polystyrene.

"Was your dad a dancer too?" (She'd seen some of my dancing results whilst stalking me on the internet. She seemed relatively impressed).

"No. Far from it. He doesn't do things."

"What things?"

"Anything."

She changed the subject, which was a relief.

"How are you getting on with Wendy? You've been together a while now."

At the mention of the name, I looked round involuntarily to see if Wendy might be lurking in the undergrowth, a fake bird upon her head and mud across her cheeks. (More likely spying on Fleur than me).

"Erm, OK I suppose."

Fleur looked me directly in the eye and for some reason my smile didn't work. It just wouldn't form on my lips.

"Can I ask you a question?"

"Of course."

"Why are you with her?"

"Because she needs me."

"Needs you how?"

I took a breath.

"Wendy isn't very nice. She's horrible to everyone. She swears at complete strangers. She nips children when she thinks no-one is looking. She wishes misfortune upon anyone that crosses her path. But I think she only does that because she's insecure and scared of being rejected. So, she hits out. I've seen it before."

"And you think you can help her?"

"Maybe. Just be nice to her, smile a lot and hope for the best."

Fleur looked at me again and I was tempted to tell her about my Project based existence. But something within me told me that I'd better not. I thought back to Dave calling me a Big Sexist and wondered if he might be right...maybe I wasn't helping these girls after all...maybe I was using them. I didn't want Fleur to think that, especially if it happened to be true.

"You're a good man Scott. But good men don't always have good ideas."

"Do you not think this is a good idea?"

"Oh, I don't know," she sighed.

We sipped at our coffee and stared into the undergrowth for a bit.

"You won't tell Wendy will you?" she asked. "About this? She would think it was weird. She'd think there was something in it."

I desperately wanted to ask "is there something in it?" It was such a screamingly obvious question. It was hanging there in the air between us, just waiting for me to pluck it. It was in my throat, on my lips. Fleur was gazing at me intently, anticipating that I would speak. But I was scared. I was scared that she'd say no. I was worried that she's just laugh and ruffle my hair or perhaps even recoil in offence. And no amount of eye gazing and bird watching and Professional Gooseberry booking could get me over that fear. So, I said nothing and she sighed and started to talk about interesting fauna.

An hour or so later, Fleur dropped me off at the same street corner and placed £20 into my hands. I tried to resist but she insisted. The Professional Gooseberry couldn't be expected to work for nothing.

"You're a good man Scott," she said as I got out of the car.

"You said that."

"I know, but I felt the need to say it again."

I walked home in my filthy plimsolls, feeling more confused, guilty and uncertain than ever.

Chapter 9

"Fail"

Project #8a – My Mum (not sure if I failed or not)

Just after I had been sacked from my first real job, my mum arrived at my front door. I was in a little house-share with a bass clarinettist and a Chinese girl called Penny. It was on that door that she knocked.

Now this was unexpected for a number of reasons, not least because I had never actually given her my address. Further, she had never been to visit me before, regardless of the address. In fact, I'm not sure she had ever visited anyone, except for her sister in Blackpool. And to add to this tale of the unexpected, she was carrying a suitcase.

"Scott," said the bass clarinettist as he stroked a chinchilla (which is not a euphemism), "there's a lady at the front door asking for you."

"A lady?" said I, perplexed at the circumstances and entranced by the way in which the bass clarinettist ran his hand up and down the furry thing's spine. I wasn't sure whether to even look.

"Yes," said the bass clarinettist in a voice as deep as his instrument.

"A sexy lady?"

"Oh yes. Oh yes indeed." The stroking intensified. "I'm going to my room now."

I went to the front door, wearing my best smile, and discovered that this sexy lady was in fact my mum. I shuddered and shouted up the stairs. "It's alright, it's just my mum."

I heard the bass clarinettist say "oh yes, oh yes indeed," as he closed his bedroom door.

I made my mum a cup of tea. It seemed the right thing to do. She made small talk as I did so; complimenting the kitchen units and the sturdiness of the stool she was perching on. I made noises in return. (I couldn't manage any words). Once she'd taken a slurp of tea, she said:

"I've come to stay for a bit."

"With me?"

"Yes."

Bloody hell, I thought, but didn't say, for fear of a parental scolding.

At this point, I should have said something compassionate and interesting like, "is everything ok?" or "can I help?" but I didn't. I should have asked "why?" I should have asked "how?" I should have asked something. I don't know why I didn't, some fear of unearthing something that I didn't want to unearth I suppose – like an archaeologist who's scared of worms.

"OK," is what I eventually said.

She drank her tea and huddled into the coat that she hadn't taken off despite the warmth of the house and the heat of the tea. She kept her battered little suitcase near her ankle and kept her gaze firmly on the floor. An uncomfortable silence, albeit not an unusual one between members of my family, stretched on.

"After you have suffered a little while, the God of all grace will himself restore you and make you strong, firm and steadfast," she said, out of nowhere.

"What was that?"

"From the Bible I think. I heard someone say it once. A long time ago."

"Oh."

I desperately searched for something else to say. Plenty of things sprang to mind but just not anything that I was actually prepared to say.

"You're just like your father," she said at one point. But even though I disagreed vehemently with that particular statement, I still couldn't bring myself to say any words.

After a while, I excused myself and went to the toilet, just for something to do. When I came back, she was gone.

Project #1 – Sally P (departed)

On Friday evenings between five and six, I used to Dance.

I would arrive home from school, exhausted and weary after a long week of academia only to be thrust into a pair of tight black trousers and what can only be described as a blouson.

I have no idea why I was obliged to attend these dance lessons, I don't recall ever expressing an initial interest in attending one. It may be that my mum decided for me; although she didn't seem to have any interest in Dance (capitalised) either. Maybe she just wanted me to work some of the fast-food-fat off of my hips.

But still, there was no question of my not going.

There was always an unusual tension in our house on a Friday evening.

I would eat my tea in silence and my mum and father would watch on, also generally in silence. Occasionally my father would pop out to answer the demands of the bell above the door in the shop and my mum would breathe a heavy breath. When he returned we would all return to our former state of muted stress.

My father must have really hated ballroom dancing.

I, on the other hand, loved it.

I was a fantastic fox-trotter, a tremendous tangoer and a wonderful waltzer. I loved it, throwing a succession of lithe, bendy little girls around a converted warehouse. And I was one of only three boys there so there was no shortage of female attention. The conditions were ripe for me to become a ladies' man of the highest order; regular, close bodily contact, desirable snake hips and substandard male competition. Podgy Lance and Camp Daniel were my love rivals. On paper, my status as the Alpha Male of the Happy Feet Dancing School was assured. In theory, I should have had a different girlfriend every week. Unfortunately, the reality was quite different as I snatched illogical singledom from the jaws of relentless relational activity. Podgy Lance and Camp Daniel on the other hand cleaned up.

I was actually quite good at the dancing though and always won the local competitions. The girls were always keen to couple with me, for that alone, as I hoovered up all the local trophies.

I remember Sally P coming to one session (before we became romantically entangled) but she was useless and never came back. The other girls laughed at her and her leg warmers. I tried to smile kindly whenever she caught my eye but she just flashed an inappropriate hand gesture at me.

My dance teacher, a ridiculously attractive and bendy woman called Ms Parker, tried to persuade my mother to allow me to extend my geographical dominance by entering the regional finals.

"He really is a wonderful dancer Mrs Logan," she would say whilst holding on to my puny little shoulders, "if he were given the freedom to dance more and enter more competitions, he could really go far. There's no end to his potential."

I yearned for my mother to agree. Something I was good at...

"My husband says he can only come once a week," my mum would say, not able to meet the eyes of Ms Parker.

"If only you would stay and watch him dance in the short hour he is here, I think you would really begin to believe in him."

"My husband says he can only come once a week."

"He dances beautifully on one hour of teaching. Imagine what he could do if he really applied himself. If it's a question of money…"

"It isn't. His father says he can only come once a week."

"Perhaps if you could bring your husband here, to see Scott dance. I don't think he's ever seen Scott dance. He might then change his mind."

"My husband never changes his mind."

Project #15 – Wendy the Worst (horrible)

The shopkeeper glared at me suspiciously and I tried to act natural. I smiled broadly, as if to say, everything is fine, this is perfectly normal, just tell me how much you need and I'll be on my way.

The shopkeeper was unconvinced by my brazen smile and left as large a gap as possible between scanning the barcode on the first Valentines' Day card and the second. Even the beep of the cash register sounded rather disapproving.

"That will be £3.59 please," the shopkeeper said as she held out a reluctant hand.

It cracked me and I blurted out… "I just can't decide which one to give to my girlfriend, they both look so nice, I just thought I'd get both. I might give her two to show her how much I love her."

My flimsy excuse was instantly batted away by the perceptive shopkeeper as she placed my 59p obligatory card into the bag next to my £3 philandering card.

I left the shop as quickly as possible but the sense of guilt was still upon me when I got home and started to write in them.

The 59p card was dealt with rather quickly:

"Wendy, words cannot express how I feel about you. Scott. X"

The £3 card for Fleur was trickier as I tried to concoct a riddle so fiendishly clever that it would both conceal my identity from the casual reader but reveal it to Fleur in a subtle way. Also, I had to write it with my left hand...in case Wendy happened to see it.

"Roses are red. Violets are blue. If Wendy finds this, she'll kill me and you."

Maybe some sort of code; a la Bletchley Park – something requiring a fiendishly clever Enigma machine to crack...

In the end, I just stopped thinking about it and wrote:

"You may not know it, but you are loved. Maybe there is something in it? X"

Under cover of darkness, I surreptitiously got the card through her letter box and sighed a deep sigh of relief.

The next morning, Valentines' Day itself, Wendy summoned me to her house so I could hand over my presents. I handed over the rather cheap card and a CD of choral music that I thought she might like.

"No flowers?" she demanded.

"Ah, no...no flowers."

She ripped open the CD and glanced at it with disdain. "I've got this."

"Oh yes, sorry."

"You should know that I have this...I play it frequently at the Work Choir."

"Oh yes," I replied meekly.

"You seem to pay more attention with the Funk Soul Family than you do at the Work Choir. You know their songs inside out. Ours, hardly at all."

"No," I demurred.

"Early to that one; late to mine. Excellent phrasing and diction there; lazy arpeggios and barely perceptible chest resonance at mine. I wonder why that is…"

She stared at me for a little while and threw the CD back at me.

"I didn't get you anything," she said.

When I got home I discovered that Fleur hadn't got me anything either.

Chapter 10

"Grammar"

Project #9 – Doreen the Dullard (successful – for both of us)

Doreen was an unusual one, in that I was never really sure whether she was a Project or not. I gave her a project number but then removed it, before reassigning it, and then taking it away again…any number of times.

Doreen was an older lady; a mature oak amongst the young saplings in my (new) office. She was an attractive older lady however and it was quite obvious that, in her heyday, she would have been quite a looker. She was rather petite and not overly loose of flesh. She was, however, loose of mind and lip.

Doreen was delightfully thick.

She thought Milton Keynes was in France and that a Water Polo team rode horses in water. She thought that only doctors could be members of parliament because she would often see that they were holding surgeries. (Get your bunion done at the same time as complaining about the frequency of green bin collections). She also swore blind that water didn't weigh anything. Genuinely.

She'd say "pacific" when she meant "specific" and "president" instead of "precedent" and she would also say "I" in any sentence, in the belief that it made her sound intelligent.

"Could you make I a coffee if you're making one?"

"Me could," I said and she'd laugh because she thought I was "being all Chinese" rather than poking fun at her.

She was one of the best workmates ever.

So when she asked me to go for a drink with her, I said yes because I thought it would be fun, not because I wanted to help her. True, she was divorced and lived alone and had no children, but it didn't seem to bother her.

She placed a drink down in front of me.

"What is that?" I asked, as I surveyed the murky concoction before me.

"A red wine spritzer."

"There's no such thing as a red wine spritzer."

"Of course there is, darling. It's there, in front of you. There's one in front of I too."

She took a sip, as if to prove that it existed.

"No, what I mean is, there is no such thing as a red wine spritzer. As a concept it doesn't exist. It's not a real thing. What even is it?"

"It's red wine and coke. Lovely darling. Tim put I on to it. You know Tim, with the funny shaped head on the second floor. He told I that it was all the rage in London, more sophisticated than a white wine spritzer. That's an old hat, he said."

She took another sip as I looked suspiciously at mine. Tim with the funny shaped head had a lot to answer for.

"Try it."

I did. And I must admit…it was disgusting.

"Do you not like it?" Doreen asked, a look of disappointment brewing on her brow.

"Of course I do," I lied…being incapable, as I am, of disappointing a woman in any circumstances other than sexual.

"Thanks for coming out Scott, it's nice of you to keep an old girl like I entertained of an evening."

"It's my pleasure. I make it a policy to say yes to attractive ladies."

Good work Scott, I said to myself. I usually think of a line like that about thirty five minutes after the opportunity to use it has passed.

"You are sweet. You remind me of my husband."

"I thought you were divorced?"

"I am, darling. Or I think I am. I'm not really sure. I left all that to him. I do remember seeing a decree something or other so it could all be done and dusted. Who knows? Who cares? Not I."

She swigged contentedly at her cocktail of ignorance and I thought to myself...this would be a good Project. To be a comfort blanket to this recently divorced woman. I could be a replacement husband of sorts. Or a surrogate child. I didn't mind which. It would actually be enjoyable. She was fun.

"Would it be rude for me to ask why you're divorced?"

"Of course not. He just got bored of I. I've always been a bit thick Scott..."

"Never!"

"I have. But I used to be pretty enough for it not to matter. My husband was never interested in my brains. He wasn't interested in a good, hard, sweaty conversation, if you get what I mean."

I did.

"I mean he just wanted to have sex with I...not talk to me."

"I had worked that out yes..."

"You see what I mean, darling, thick as too short plants, I am."

"But you're still very sexy..." I ventured, mining my recently discovered flirtatious gold. I even raised an eyebrow...

"Oh, you are sweet. I'm alright I suppose for an old bird. But he wasn't interested when I started to sag you-know-where; or when my bingo wings started flapping when I was doing the you-know-what. He traded me in as they say. Sorry, he traded I in."

"For shame!" I exclaimed.

"He did. And if you think I'm thick, you ought to see her. She still has Velcro on her shoes."

I laughed at that, having used that very line myself when trying to impress old Nicola Big Nose. Perhaps old Doreen was trying to impress me?

When it was time for another drink, I made sure I was first to the bar.

"What's this?"

"It's a deconstructed red wine spritzer," I explained.

"That sounds fancy," she said as she took a sip of red wine whilst I made a start on the coca cola.

"I've been looking you up Scott, on the internet."

"Have you? Why?"

"I always look people up on the internet nowadays, make sure they're genuine. People tell lies Scott; terrible lies. I once had a relationship with a man who told me he was the British ambassador to Bangladesh."

I could see where this was going – poor old thick-but-still-sexy Doreen would be spun a line by any sexual cad and bounder.

"And let me guess, it turned out he was a boiler repair man from Felixstowe…"

"Oh no, worse than that, he was just a cultural attaché.

"Right…" I said, having been well and truly stumped, "so what did you find when you looked me up?"

"I found that you'd got your own website."

Damn.

"The Professional Gooseberry. No situation is too embarrassing. No atmosphere is too tense. If you need a Plus One or an extra bum on a spare seat, I'm your man."

"I should probably tell you that I didn't really get much business."

"Well, you have now. I'd like to book you."

"You want to book me?" I asked. "What for?"

"To be my gooseberry."

"Why?"

"Because I'm a fifty three year old divorcee and sometimes you just need someone."

And so began one of the most pleasant periods of my professional life as a gooseberry. She took me to the local dry ski slope. I accompanied her around a farm shop and picked out some asparagus. I took her car to the garage for its annual service. I baked a cake with her one Sunday afternoon; a jam and cream sponge. I went to a few dinner parties where I was permitted to talk. All at slightly above the national minimum wage.

But, truth be told, I did feel a little guilty about my relationship with Doreen; so much so that eventually I had to break it off. It wasn't the money so much, in that I knew she could afford it - her ex-husband had paid her off in quite spectacular fashion. It was just that Doreen never seemed to really understand the concept of the professional gooseberry and I felt I was taking advantage of her stupidity, or her naivety, or her good nature, or just of her cheque book.

When we went to the dry ski slope, I wasn't actually needed, as we met up with a group of her friends. In fact, Doreen went to the dry ski slope every Monday night with the same group of friends – all of whom were accomplished skiers who partook of regular Alpine jaunts. I, on the other hand, spent the entire evening on the baby slope, falling over every thirty seconds or so. I only saw Doreen at the end of the night over a restorative half pint of ale.

One of her friends, Jeb, said encouragingly: "Don't worry mate, it gets easier. I don't think the Chinese have many dry ski slopes."

I was about to respond with my familiar refrain when I caught a glimpse of myself in a blackened window...looking fairly oriental by any objective standard. It must have been the ski goggles.

When I took her car in for its service, I took it on my own. Doreen was busy; meeting a girlfriend for coffee and cake. I just picked up the car from her house, took it to the garage, waited around and then filled in the required amount on a pre-signed cheque. That wasn't exactly how the Professional Gooseberry was supposed to function. It was more of a dogsbody function – an entirely different type of website.

And when I went to a dinner party at her house; attended by a group of her old school friends, Doreen introduced me:

"Oh by the way, this is Scott. He's a professional gooseberry. I'm paying him to be here."

I smiled that one out and hoped people didn't notice the reddening of my face.

As it happens, they were very interested in my professional capacity and I thought I might get some business out of it until I realised that most of the other dinner party attendees had also misunderstood the essential features of the P.G – making enquiries, as they did, about my availability for dog walking and whether I'd be free on Thursday morning to wait in for a parcel.

After everyone had left and Doreen had handed me a small packet of money I gave my notice.

"You're quitting?"

"I am. I think the old gooseberry has had its day."

"Oh, that's a shame."

"There is a season for everything…"

"Well, at least I can say I've helped you," she said with a gracious smile.

"You've helped me?" I asked.

"Yes, darling."

"I thought I was helping you."

"I don't need help little darling. I'm as happy as Larry. I just wanted to make you happy for a bit."

"Me? Happy?" I had to laugh. "I'm notorious for being one of the happiest, most optimistic, genial people alive. It really annoys people in the office. You've heard people call me Smiley Scott haven't you?"

"Oh yes, I know you smile all the time. But you only smile with your mouth – not your eyes darling. Never your eyes."

So maybe Doreen wasn't so thick after all.

Project #1 – Sally Paxton (gone)

Sally placed a folded up piece of paper into my hand as I got on the school bus. It had been folded as many times as is physically possible (which I think is seven) and it took me a while to open it when I got a seat.

"What's that, a love letter?" said Dave as he leered over my shoulder. I quickly thrust it in my pocket before he could grab it – that was the kind of thing he would do.

"Shut up Dave," I said.

"Hey, everyone," Dave shouted to get the attention of our fellow passengers on the bus. "Old Second Hand here has a got a love letter from Shaggy Paxton."

He tried to start a whoop but it didn't catch on.

When I finally got some privacy I re-opened the letter. It was a poem of sorts:

"You are my globe and I am your snow."

That was it. I wasn't sure whether she'd run out of poetic inspiration or simple motivation. Either way, I was bemused and touched in equal measure.

I mentioned it to my mum when my father was in the toilet.

"Does she mean we're interdependent? Inseparable? That you can't have one without the other? Does it mean I'm her world? Or that she's inside me? Or that she brings movement to an otherwise dull scene?"

My mum took a minute to absorb my diatribe, a faraway look in her eyes.

"Maybe it means she feels trapped…" she said.

Project #15 – Wendy the Worst (demanding)

I was supposed to be writing a poem. Wendy had told me that she wanted a poem and that I had to write it. It was to be romantic and loving but with deep undertones of sexuality. I wasn't entirely sure how I was going to do that with the words that happened to rhyme with "Wendy." So far, I had only finished a line that ended with "bendy" and was trying desperately to segue into something about being "trendy."

Besides being a complete poetical numpty, the main problem was that I found myself thinking about Fleur. Not only did her name have more accessible rhymes – buerre, cur, fur, were – it also had a lyricism about it in itself. Just saying the name over and over again was a poem.

"Oh Fleur, Fleur, Fleur…"

That was the best line I came up with all day.

The problem had started when Fleur had arrived at choir practice carrying a book of poetry.

"What is this?" demanded Wendy as she snatched the book out of Fleur's hand. She didn't wait for an answer. "It's a book of poetry."

I went into an immediate internal panic…rotating of bowels, hammering of heart.

"Yes, it is, can I have it back please?" Fleur asked calmly as she put out her hand.

"Do you like poetry?" Wendy demanded once more, suspicious. "I didn't know you liked poetry."

"I have started to like it recently."

I knew the moment that Fleur had started to like poetry was the very moment I had placed a book of love poems in to her hand (just in the way that one friend hands another friend a book of love poetry). If Wendy happened to look just inside the front cover, she would know it too. Fleur had not mentioned the Valentine's Card that I had put through her door. She hadn't even given me an extra special look. I started to wonder whether she knew who it was from. Maybe I had been too abstract. I therefore took the rather bold step of handing a book of love poetry to Fleur as I passed her in the corridor at work.

"What's this?" she asked.

"Just a book that I thought you might like. It says things."

"What things?"

"Important things."

Fleur wandered off in a rather bemused manner and I again puzzled over whether I had been too abstract. But I thought the fact that I had seen her carrying the book of poetry around the office was a good sign.

"I like poetry too," said Wendy. "I like all the greats – Tennyson, Wordsmith, Bryon..."

"Yes, me too," said Fleur.

Wendy sidled closer to Fleur and whispered gently; but not gently enough...as I heard.

"I may have written a poem about you once or twice. Erotic imagery throughout. Sensual couplets. I could make these available if they might be of interest?"

Fleur clearly didn't know what to say. Wendy gave her a wink and resumed her normal voice.

"What about you Scott, do you like poetry?" Wendy stared at me – as if she knew that I did.

"I don't really know much about it," I lied.

There was something in the air at that moment; suspicion, doubt, distrust. But eventually Wendy passed the book back to Fleur, making sure her fingers brushed Fleur's palm.

"You should learn something about poetry Scott. It's becoming of a man. You shall write something for me."

So there I was trying to write something that would ensure that Wendy wouldn't overly tweak my nipples the next time we engaged in coitus, at the same time as trying to ensure that my proclamations of love were benign enough not to upset Fleur – who I knew was the eventual target of the completed poem. Wendy wanted to give Fleur a poem but perhaps thought an erotic limerick might be a step too far, so she had subcontracted the work to me.

"Make it generalised…don't use my name…make it about a woman; any woman – it needn't be me but it should be me."

Those had been my less than clear instructions. I assumed Wendy was going to pass off my work as her own – which is why I had gone rogue and tried to weave a "bendy Wendy" reference in there somewhere. (Although I knew I would probably take it out later).

My phone rang. I groaned and answered it. It was Dave.

"Alright poofter," he said.

"Hello Dave, what's up?"

I'm gagging for a kebab so it must be my time to visit you again. Beers, birds and kebab; what more can a young, single man like myself want?"

"Has she left you then?"

"Yes. Went this morning. Bit of an overreaction I thought. I mean, she said that she wanted me to get on well with her family. I said that to her actually when she found me in bed with her sister, "you wanted me to get on well with your family." Do you get it? I don't think she got it because she just threw an alarm clock at me and ran off."

"Why do you do it Dave? I thought you said this one was different."

"Well, she was. I could have lived most of my life with her. But then I met the sister."

"And what was she? Stunning I suppose? Turned your head?"

"Not really, quite ugly actually, but gagging for it, totally gagging for it. I just had to...anyway, I thought I'd come down and we can drown our sorrows and then chat up some birds and I can get my end away as usual and you can go home on your own."

"If you must."

"Anyway, I'm looking forward to seeing what sort of basket case you're rehabilitating at the moment."

Chapter 11

"Grin"

Project #10 – Kay the Kougar (successful – damn)

I can only imagine that Doreen had been talking about me around the office; that's the only explanation really for what happened with Kay.

Kay was the most senior member of our team – in terms of years rather than position – and was responsible for dealing with customer complaints. At her most placid and relaxed Kay's face looked rather like a scrunched up walnut. When she was on the phone to a complaining customer, the said walnut became red and inflamed as rage and exasperation flowed out of Kay's soul and into her face. She was famed for using the phrase, "with all due respect," just before delivering the most cutting and terse of insults down the phone.

"With all due respect, if your son is stupid enough to fall into an extremely well-marked hole then I don't hold out much hope for his future, never mind his claim for compensation."

Her words, and the way in which she used them, generated a phenomenal number of complaints – but due to staff shortages all complaints about Kay were directed to Kay so very few of them were ever upheld. Kay did actually uphold one or two a year, just to give the appearance of impartiality in the end of year figures.

The end of each call would generally be followed by the phrase, "God help us." It was Kay's way of saying that everyone in the world was a cretin – except her.

Every now and then, some member of senior management would seek to solve the Kay Conundrum – i.e., how to sack her. But she would just go on long term sick leave (severe gout of the big toe) until the senior manager got bored and went away to bother someone else.

Her return to work usually resulted in a sharp dip in morale.

But other than that, I suppose she was quite nice.

I never really had anything to do with her; except for one day when she stood outside the office handing out leaflets (in contravention of the company's apolitical policy) to promote the local Green Party candidate in the upcoming local council elections.

"Do you care about the polar ice caps Scott?"

"I do."

"In which case, can I count on you to vote green?"

"Maybe."

"Don't you care about the butterflies Scott?"

"I do."

"What about wasps?"

"Less so."

"Wasps are very important to the eco system. The Conservative candidate doesn't care about wasps. The Labour candidate doesn't care about wasps. The Liberal Democrat candidate doesn't care about wasps. They only care about buses and hospitals and bin collections. Can I count on your vote Scott?"

"Can I think about it?" I asked, smiling as broadly as possible to deflect any potential disappointment.

"What more persuasion do you need?"

"I just want to look at the holistic picture."

"God help us," she said as she rolled her eyes and tried to collar someone else.

As it happens I didn't vote Green and I suspect that Kay knew that and held it against me. Not that she was any ruder to me than she was to anyone else in the office. So, when Kay sent me an email to ask me to meet her for a coffee in order to discuss a private matter, I was intrigued and slightly scared.

When I arrived at the designated coffee shop Kay was smiling, which was odd in itself. The smile looked wrong on her face. She then bought the drinks and even offered to buy me a muffin if I was so inclined. I was so inclined and tucked into a blueberry muffin as Kay cleared her throat a number of times. She was something approaching nervous, I observed.

"I've been speaking to Doreen," she began.

"Oh yes?"

"She tells me that you like to help people."

"I do."

"Girls, mainly."

"Yes."

"Doreen said you'll do anything to help a girl. Build her confidence. Keep her busy. Improve her self-esteem, that sort of thing."

"That's it exactly. Second Hand Scott they call me."

"I thought that was because you never have original thoughts? You just recycle what other people say."

"No..." I said, rather put out by that. *I have lots of original thoughts*, I thought.

"Right," Kay said, rather uncertainly.

I finished my blueberry muffin and wondered what sort of proposition Kay might have for me. A beautiful yet painfully shy granddaughter? A nymphomaniac niece? A divorced middle aged daughter in need of comfort and companionship?

"Is there anything I can help you with?"

"Yes there is..." said Kay as I shivered with the excitement that only a new Project can bring, "...sex."

Now we're talking.

"Sex?"

"Yes, sex. With me."

Damn.

"Sex?" I repeated again.

"Yes Scott, sex."

"Sex?" The ground seemed to be rushing towards me from various angles. I was hoping the sugar from the blueberry muffin would kick in soon otherwise I was going to pass out.

"God help us. Yes, sex. Intercourse. Having it off. A damn good rogering. Whatever you want to call it, I need it and I was hoping you might deliver it."

I wasn't entirely sure what to say. Nothing I had ever seen or heard had prepared me for a situation such as thus: to be sexually propositioned by a saucy old age pensioner.

"I'm due to retire early next year and once I do my chances of having sexual intercourse with anyone outside of the Green Party will be non-existent. Not that I would have sex with any of the men in the local membership – many of them don't even wash."

"Aren't you about eighty?"

I should have added, "with all due respect" but was too shocked.

"I am barely sixty seven. But I still have needs."

"Needs?"

"Truth be told Scott, I haven't had a sniff of anything since my husband died twenty three years ago."

"Sixty seven?" I said, feeling faint.

"Don't be ageist as well as sexist Scott, it's not an enviable characteristic. Not in this day and age – no pun intended. I can still perform my duties in the bedroom if you can withstand them."

I lifted a shaky hand and took a sip of my coffee.

"And let me tell you, my husband was not disappointed with my efforts between the sheets. He died with a smile on his face. I will literally do anything – nothing too perverse or degrading. I'll show you things that you didn't even know existed."

I spat out my coffee.

Project #1 – Sally P (lifeless)

Sally Paxton auditioned for one of the lead roles in the school production of Half a Sixpence. She'd sung with gusto, acted with conviction and danced with fluidity – and then got a part in the Chorus alongside some of the Special Needs Children. She was naturally disappointed and pushed a fire extinguisher off the wall when she got the news.

I was given the role of Principal Dancer in the production; meaning I would be front and centre for all the big numbers. Sally P was somewhere near the back, next to one of the curtains, but I thought she might at least enjoy looking at my jiggling bottom. The role of Principal Dancer has been especially created for me; in an effort to persuade my mum to allow me to take part in the show. She had shown initial reluctance, but the rather impressive sounding title of Principal Dancer was enough to sway her.

My relationship with Sally P was in its early stages when we started rehearsals. We hadn't really struck up much of a romantic rapport or even a relational routine. In fact, I'd barely seen her or spoken to her. She tended to ignore me around school; which I put down to shyness. I thought the school production might be the perfect opportunity to get to know her. Alas, it wasn't to be. I did my best to be the epitome of the devoted, interested boyfriend but my duties as Principal Dancer meant that sometimes I was called upon to jiggle onstage for long periods of time.

Meanwhile, Sally P was often to be found in the boys' changing rooms, or sometimes she'd be found in a small cupboard with the adolescents responsible for the stage lighting, or sometimes she'd be found outside on the grass sharing the same cigarette with the school caretaker.

But whenever I had a moment, I would track her down.

I also gave her as much help as I could with the tricky choreography from the show. It's not altogether easy to throw your hands up in the air and shout "cheese" at the same time, and Sally P struggled quite significantly with any sort of multi-tasking, despite the feminine cliché.

Dave, who had also got himself into the production in the hope of getting to know some of the "arty" girls in school ("I've done all the ones from P.E."), joked about Sally P's lack of synchronicity one break time, saying, "I've seen her do a couple of things at once no problem, if you know what I mean…" and I almost punched him in the mouth – and would have actually punched him in the mouth but for the knowledge that Dave was bigger, stronger and tougher than me and would not hesitate to punch me back – best friend or no.

Despite the rehearsal period being fairly tricky for me, the show itself was a triumph. Our lead actors could act, our lead singers could sing, and our lead dancer – or should I say Principal Dancer – could dance the back legs off a specially trained dancing poodle.

The local newspaper said the show was a "joyous, thrilling piece de resistance."

My father read the write-up in the local paper but didn't comment, perhaps because he didn't know what a piece de resistance was. I thought my mum was going to cry when she read it, even though I'm pretty sure that she didn't know what a piece de resistance was either.

My mum even went so far as to discuss the situation with my father:

"His teacher says he should go and study dance somewhere…after school… professionally…it needn't be like when I…"

But my father had to abruptly leave the room at that point so I'm not sure if the conversation was ever finished.

The show was so good that the Headmistress of our school decided to throw a party after the final show. A "wrap party" I believe they call it in the Business of Show. Truth be told, it wasn't much of a party. Cocktail sausages and a compilation of 80s chart hits playing through the Tannoy system in the school hall does not a party make. Neither did seeing Sally Paxton (my girlfriend) kissing another boy in the middle of the dance floor during "99 Red Balloons" – in full view of everyone.

Project #15 – Wendy & Fleur (optional)

The Funk Soul Family didn't get many gigs; it was mainly charity nights and the occasional community function where we could be counted upon to perform for free. (There were 37 of us, so quite an expensive booking had we charged by the person). But we were asked to sing a Christmas Carol or two when the local seasonal lights were turned on.

We were tremendous, both musically and stylistically; although I'm not sure that the huddled mass of frost-bitten seasonal late-night shoppers were quite ready for a funk / soul version of "O Little Town of Bethlehem." And when we added a funk / soul beat to Cliff Richards' "Mistletoe and Wine" a section of elderly shoppers stropped off in what I could only interpret as disgust. However, a couple of men near the front of the stage seemed to enjoy it, inaccurately swaying and whooping to the beat – although they were quite clearly the worse for drink.

We had been introduced onto the stage by a talking monkey (via a ventriloquist) and the lights were switched on by one of the disc jockeys from the local radio station. He caused quite a stir by saying a rude word in an unguarded moment. No-one was offended though as the section of society most likely to be offended by such a thing had already left when the Funk Soul Family mangled Cliff's seasonal favourite. The back-stage area (a gazebo) had an unending supply of mulled wine and mince pies. There was a general sense of seasonal bonhomie about the whole place. And when the Christmas lights went on, well, even the most cynical observer would have to admit that they were beautiful.

All in all it had the makings of a great night...but for me, it was purgatory.

Wendy was there, which didn't help, but that wasn't the reason for the raging torrent of jealousy and hatred in my bosom.

Fleur had brought a man.

"You remind me of that monkey," Wendy said to me as we watched a grown man prance about the stage with his hand up a primate's bottom.

"Do I?"

"Compliant. Willing. Manoeuvrable."

"I'll take that as a compliment."

"I wouldn't. It isn't."

(I had detected a cooling in Wendy's attitude towards me since I gave her my poem. She wasn't taken by it).

Prior to the show and whilst Wendy was arguing with the artistic director of the Funk Soul Family about whether "O Little Town" would best suit a reggae or a calypso beat, I scanned the tent for Fleur. She was nowhere to be seen. That was quite unlike her – pleasant people are usually punctual. I hoped she was OK.

I passed the time of day with a few of my Funk Soul brothers and sisters, casually asking whether Fleur was ill or on holiday or otherwise engaged. No-one seemed to know anything. Wendy had cornered the local radio disc jockey in one angle of the tent and was squeezing his biceps through his coat.

"Hi Scott."

At last...! I would know that pleasant sounding voice anywhere. I took a breath of joyful anticipation and turned in the hope of spending just a few small minutes with Fleur whilst Wendy tried to force her affections on the DJ.

But Fleur was not alone.

Fleur was standing next to a man. In fact, she had her arm looped through his and she was standing far too close to him. I immediately and thoroughly hated this man; with his tallness and his nicely cut hair and his pleasant smile and his warm, woolly coat and his shoulders which were touching Fleur. (That was our thing – we touched shoulders on a regular basis as we sang. It wasn't decent to touch shoulders with more than one man on a regular basis).

I smiled; the grin on my face no more genuine than the smirk sewn on to the face of that bloody monkey.

"This is my friend, Leonard."

Leonard. My friend. My friend. Leonard.

"Hi, nice to meet you," he said, giving me a little wave from all of half a metre.

What a total bastard.

Leonard offered his hand but before I could even think about shaking it, Wendy was there with her firm handshake.

"In my day, disc jockeys of any variety were perverts. They'd do anything to anyone. But that poor excuse of man over there says he's got two kids and a lovely wife called Annabel and would rather just turn the lights on and get on home. Disgraceful. Who are you?"

The last was directed to Leonard, with whom she was still shaking hands.

"This is Leonard..." began Fleur.

"Her friend," I blurted out.

"A friend with benefits I'll wager," said Wendy. "Well, can't blame you Fleur, he's a good looking man. He could have my womanhood any day of the week."

At that moment, I did have a smidge of pity for Leonard – he didn't know how to respond to such brazen vulgarity - but I crushed it immediately owing to the fact that he looked at Fleur in his discomfort – and their eyes met. That was our thing.

As we sang our songs on the stage near the Christmas tree, all the thrill of the performance was subsumed by supreme jealousy. It was the highlight of my week to stand next to Fleur on the back row of the choir, bumping shoulders and just enjoying each other's presence. If I tilted my shoulders slightly to the right, I could almost pretend that Wendy wasn't on the other side of me. It was bliss. Usually.

But not that night…it was hell.

Fleur (the girl to whom I had given a book of love poetry, the girl who had booked the Professional Gooseberry) spent the entire gig smiling into the crowd – towards Leonard. And I could see that he was smiling back. Fleur, perhaps subconsciously, compressed her shoulder blades and halted the natural sway of her hips, meaning that we didn't touch once throughout the entire show. Not once. And if I happened to glance to the other side, I noticed Wendy sharing her sensual gazes between Leonard, the petrified disc jockey and the side of Fleur's head. (None of which were returned).

"….time to rejoice in the good that we see…"

Cliff's well-meaning words felt flat on my tongue.

Chapter 12

"Mercy"

Project #11 – Melinda the Merciless (Successful)

A few months after my encounter with Kay – after the tremors had subsided and the nightmares had started to fade – Melinda from reception sat next to me in the office canteen.

"Hello mate," she said, "mind if I sit down?"

Melinda called everyone "mate." I was never sure whether Melinda used the term "mate" as a genuine term of endearment, or whether her eyesight was so bad that she daren't hazard a guess at a name. Melinda was highly bespectacled.

"Of course," I said.

Melinda put her face almost in my plate of food.

"Meatballs?" Melinda said without withdrawing her face. "I love meatballs. Big balls of meat. Meaty, meaty balls of meat. Can't beat them can you mate?"

"Would you like them?" I offered, as she was virtually eating them anyway.

"No thanks...got me a salad."

Melinda stopped looking at my food and started to poke about at the fare on her plate. She kept trying to skewer a small kernel of sweet corn without success. At first, I put this down to her chronically bad eyesight but after a moment or two, I realised it was more likely to be agitation.

"You like meatballs then?" she asked after a few moments.

"I do."

"Can't beat them. Meat. Balls."

My sixth sense suddenly told me that Melinda was not sitting next to me by accident; nor was she so excited by my menu choice that she kept repeating herself. She was nervous. She was building up to something.

Like many of the women in my life, nerves were not one of the things commonly associated with Melinda. Nor was the concept of building up to something. Melinda was a "think it, do it" kind of person with a penchant for the immediate.

Melinda was known as Melinda the Merciless around the office; not because she was horrible – quite the opposite really, she was always very pleasant, what with her "mate this" and "mate that" – but because she worked on reception and was a stickler for the rules. As the guardian of the gate (into work) she was a relentless sentinel of the security policy…if you didn't have your pass, you weren't getting in.

It didn't matter who you were…office junior, photocopier repair man, the managing director…if you didn't have your pass, she wouldn't buzz you through the door. End of story.

"Sorry mate," she'd say, "it's the rules."

It was particularly entertaining one time when the Chief Executive came out of the building after a long, hard day of doing whatever it is that Chief Executives do, and then tried to get back in to get his pass which he had left on his desk.

"Can't let you in mate, you've got no pass."

"But I've just come out. You saw me. I'm the Chief Executive"

"That's as may be, but I can't let you in without a pass."

"But I need to get in to get my pass…"

"If you want to go in to get your pass you'll need a pass."

Melinda the Merciless would often then open a magazine until whichever exasperated applicant went away. The poor old Chief Executive just watched her in supreme agitation as she checked the T.V. listings. After a while he started shouting, but she turned to the horoscopes.

The next day the Chief Executive investigated whether there was a way to sack Melinda but decided that firing someone for complying with a policy that the Chief Executive had introduced might be a little odd – so she survived.

I had heard that story third or fourth hand and wasn't sure it was true until I once forgot my security pass and tried to get into the office by casually waving a supermarket loyalty card in front of her eyes. She wasn't fooled by my nonchalance however and reported me to Human Resources for "attempted fraud." (Which was a bit of an exaggeration).

"What's on your mind Melinda?"

She looked me directly in the eye.

"That obvious eh mate?"

"I have a sixth sense for women who want something from me…what is it?"

"I hear you help people…?"

"Who have you been speaking to?"

Please not Kay, please not Kay, please not Kay.

"Doreen…we do Zumba together."

Phew.

"It's true. That's why they call me Second Hand Scott."

"Oh, I thought that was because you were a bit of a gossip?"

How rude! And entirely untrue.

"No it isn't…what do you need?"

"Nothing really. Nothing much. I just want someone to spend my birthday with."

I scrunched my wary eyes…memories of being sexually ambushed by Kay floating into my suspicious mind.

"When you say, "spend"…?"

"Oh nothing like that, you saucy sod. Just dinner, a movie, something like that, something to make me feel special. I kicked my husband out you see, a year or two back because he…well, we needn't go into that…I was well within my rights. And I haven't got anyone to spend the day with. I thought you could be a mate."

I did take her to a movie and I did take her to dinner. I even bought her a little present. (A candle). She pretended to like it and when I dropped her off at home after our dinner date she gave me a little kiss on the cheek and said:

"Thanks Scott, that's really cheered me up. You're a gentleman."

Project #1 – Sal P (not here)

It took me quite a long time to write the letter. I sat at a small metal table in the back of the shop and agonised over the correct choice of words.

"You're dumped," would have probably done the trick but it didn't have enough poetry to it. Too blunt, too imprecise.

I wasn't exactly dumping her; I was letting her go, giving up, admitting defeat. I needed to convey that. It wasn't that she had let *me* down by kissing Alex Simpson in full view of everyone at school; it was that she had let *herself* down. (And she had let me down).

I wanted to convey that I thought she had the capacity – the potential – to be a beautiful person. To be a woman who commanded respect. A woman of choice and self-determination. But that she couldn't do that whilst she floated around, kissing Alex Simpsons and sharing cigarettes with caretakers…doing whatever anyone wanted her to do in order to gain some form of social approval.

And even as I sat there I realised I was being tremendously patronising – which made the letter even more difficult to write. (Fancy taking advice on social integration and personal integrity from a boy who smiles all the time and can't say no). But still, I soldiered on. How to be paternal without being patronising? Quandary.

"Dad...?" I asked with an elongated vowel.

My father was busy stacking polystyrene cups. He raised an eyebrow at me.

"...have you ever broken up with a girl in such a way that conveys that you're not doing it out of choice, but rather that you feel compelled to do it in the best interests of the girl...and that the said girl will always hold a place of affection in your heart as you wish her well for the future?"

My father shook his head and left the room.

"Mum, any ideas?"

My mum was busy filling in some sort of book – perhaps an account ledger.

"Sorry dear?"

"I was just asking if you've got any experience of breaking up with someone? Ending a relationship."

My mother stared off into space for a while...

"Sorry little one, I don't."

I turned back to the blank page and continued to agonise; my parents having been of no use whatsoever. I don't know why I was putting so much effort into a break up letter. Sally P had hardly put any effort into our relationship.

We'd only been together for a few weeks and in that time I'd only seen her twice (properly seen her I mean – not counting glimpses at school or the shenanigans during the school production). She'd invited me up to her bedroom for our first "date"...which, as you can imagine for a fifteen year old boy, was tremendously exciting (particularly given the rumour that Sally P had a red light bulb up there), but all she did was show me the lyrics to a song she had been writing; fifteen pages of verse, chorus, verse, chorus, bridge, etc – all of it utter bilge. It was all throbbing regret and bulbous pity tied in with far too many references to a Cross Dressing Lucifer and the Angel of Death wearing leather trousers. I could barely read it; such was its inane drivel-like quality.

I told her I liked it though and she squeezed my hand really hard.

The second time I saw her (properly I mean) she met me at the indoor market in town and I followed her round as she talked to a succession of market stall holders; all of whom seemed to know her quite well. She would chat for a little while and then ask if she could have something for free. We managed to get a couple of apples, a novelty lighter and some pipe cleaners as a reward for our efforts.

"I'm good at getting what I want," she said.

That was it; the sum total of our relationship.

I asked her out. She said yes. I glimpsed her a few times around school. In our shop. She invited me to her bedroom to read some truly horrendous lyrical vomit. We bothered some market stall holders. And then she kissed Alex Simpson at the Half a Sixpence after party.

So, why was I putting so much effort into that bloody letter?

When Dave came round (somewhere around teatime as usual) I was still working on it, even if my working area had been gradually squeezed by my father as he placed sacks of potatoes and bowls of batter around me.

"Just put something like, "I only went out with you for the shag but you were rubbish at that anyway, so I'm dumping you.""

Dave settled down to a tray of chips and gravy with a look of satisfied smugness about him; as if Oscar Wilde couldn't have put it any better.

"I didn't "shag" her."

Dave nearly choked on a chip.

"But you've been going out with her for weeks."

"I know."

"But…"

"I didn't go out with her for the sex," I said in a quiet voice as my father was rather too close for comfort, stirring some peas.

"What else is there with Shaggy Paxton?"

"I don't like you calling her that. She is my girlfriend you know."

"Yeah, until she reads that letter."

I sighed an exasperated sigh and ripped another piece of paper from my pad.

"I'm trying to find some form of words that will stay with her for the rest of her life; some sort of positive reinforcement even as I deliver the crushing news. Basically, I'm trying to change her for the better."

"Sexist, told you."

"Shut up Dave."

"How about...roses are red, violets are blue, you didn't put out so I'm dumping you."

"Get lost Dave."

"Ah, just get on with it and I'll post it through her letter box on my way home."

Project #15 – Wendy & Fleur (different)

"How would you describe your attitude to sexuality Scott?"

Wendy and I were sitting in the coffee bar at work one lunchtime. This had quickly become our usual routine. She made me meet her there for a Panini and a mineral water for a number of consecutive days until I just started to turn up there automatically. I think farmers associate similar routines with cattle.

We always sat in the same pair of seats. She would get there early to make sure no-one else could have them. (I was never entirely sure what Wendy did for a job but her hours seemed to be self-regulating. Her boss was probably terrified of her). She would then ask me outrageous questions at maximum volume so that everyone in the coffee bar would hear.

"To what extent would you consider yourself legitimately racially prejudiced?"

"How should we deal with the gypsy problem?"

"What percentage of disability is faked?"

I wouldn't even get the opportunity to answer. These questions were rhetorical set-ups; asked purely for the purpose of allowing Wendy to speak at length – as if she were on some sort of rostrum. She'd just go off on one, or two, or thirty-seven. I just smiled and sipped my mineral water and tried not to look at Fleur.

Fleur, delightful, lovely, gorgeous Fleur, worked just adjacent to the coffee bar. Wendy, it seems, had chosen these particular seats for two reasons. Firstly because she could get a good look at Fleur as we drank our mineral water and secondly, because at 1pm every single working day, Fleur would get herself a cappuccino. Wendy chose the moments when Fleur was standing in the queue, payment and loyalty card at the ready, as the moment to deliver an extreme opinion.

In some deranged portion of Wendy's mind, she thought this might be impressive.

"The thing about me Scott," she would say very loudly, "is that I do not have a prejudicial bone in my body. How can I have when I am so sexually pliable? Besides, I have lots of black friends. Well, when I say friends, I mean people I buy goods and services from, but I am on first name terms with the ones who wear name badges. In fact, I am so lacking in prejudice that this allows me to analyse and rationalise certain issues without fear of my judgment being clouded by partiality or political correctness. Are you following me…?"

As it happens, I wasn't. I'd been thinking of a time when I'd come third in the local salsa championships with a girl called Benjamina Bhutan. (Stage name – I can't remember her real name). I'd accidentally stood on her toe, causing her to stumble and costing us victory, and she had never spoken to me again. Ms Bhutan was really quite horrible, so the cold shoulder was a welcome relief. I don't know why I happened to be thinking about that at that precise moment.

"...so when I ask the question of whether a large proportion of those claiming disability are faking, you can be assured that I have no pre-conceived notions of how the question should be answered. But take my parents, they never had a day off despite..."

I drifted off again as I watched Fleur pay for her cappuccino. She smiled at the counter assistant and proffered her little loyalty card which was duly stamped. I wanted to stamp her loyalty card, and that wasn't a euphemism.

Wendy always asked, as Fleur was squeezing the plastic lid on to her takeaway cup:

"Ah Fleur, I didn't see you there. Won't you join us? We're discussing politics. I know you're interested in social issues..."

Fleur always answered: "Sorry, would love to, but must get back."

Back to send an email to bloody Leonard bloody boyfriend..

She smiled at me as she left. My smile slipped for a moment.

"I don't think she can bear to see us together," said Wendy as Fleur returned to her desk.

Chapter 13

"Character"

Project #12 - Rita the Ridiculous (successful)

The first time I met Rita, she was dressed as a turkey.

I was standing in a queue in the staff room at work, desperately hoping that the lemon drizzle cake wouldn't disappear before I got to the front. The two old dears in front of me in the queue were taking an age to decide.

"Ooo, so much choice…"

I was mentally urging them towards the Victoria sponge. I was concentrating so hard on trying to cerebrally influence this indecisive duo that I didn't notice Rita as she shuffled into the staff room dressed as fowl.

Truth be told, I wasn't exactly dressed in the stereotypical business / office fashion myself; sporting as I did a red and white striped jumper with a half-eaten gingerbread man on it. The two old dears in front of me were wearing droopy Santa hats and the man behind me was wearing a knitted sweatshirt with the post-ironic statement "bah humbug" emblazoned upon it. But a full turkey costume, giblets included, was excessive even for an office "dress-down" day.

Rita shuffled and squawked herself straight to the front of the queue.

"Mind out, I haven't got long to live. Need some cake before they chop my head off!"

The droopy delayers were edged away from the table by Rita's feathery, flapping arms.

"I'll just take these..." Rita said as she dragged the whole table of cakes towards the door, causing the donation pot to spill on the ground.

"What am I like? You cannot take me anywhere. Well, they knew what I was like when they employed me. I told them at my interview, "I'm mad me!""

Once order had been restored (by the old dears) and Rita had stopped laughing at her own jokes and I'd managed to get my mitts on some lemon drizzle, I followed Rita out into the corridor.

"I like your outfit," I said – just in case she'd seen the evil stare the man in the "bah humbug" jumper had given her.

"What outfit? This isn't fancy dress you know, I always wear this on a Friday."

She guffawed at her own joke. Again. I smiled politely.

"You know what would be hilarious?" she said once she'd stop guffawing.

"What?"

"If we went out for a drink after work, dressed like this. You can just imagine what the locals would make of us two. They wouldn't know what to do. They'd be like, "whoa, a crazy man in a gingerbread jumper has just walked into the pub with a life size turkey!""

"Would they?"

"Of course they would. It's not everyday you see a giant turkey walk into your local pub is it?"

A few minutes after work, as we stood on the threshold of the local pub, Rita said, "if someone asks me why I'm dressed as a turkey, I'm just going to pretend I don't know what they're talking about, totally deadpan, as if I'm just dressed normally and they're seeing things. They'll be like, "whoa, how drunk am I?" It will be totally hilarious."

After she'd finished guffawing again (there really is no other word for it), we made our way to the bar, entirely unmolested by disbelieving titters. The barmaid didn't even blink an eyelid as she asked, "what can I get you?"

For the next few hours, Rita regaled me with stories of derring-do and madcappery from her hectic and crazy life. She'd once played the part of a bat in an amateur stage show musical and hung upside for so long that she passed out half way through the first act. She'd married a guy she'd just met in Las Vegas and had never seen him again. (She was technically still married). She'd got some ill-advised tattoos, one of a gherkin (the vegetable thing, not the tall building). She had attempted a tightrope walk across a waterfall but had fallen in after about three steps. She'd appeared in a burlesque show with a number of dwarfs, some of whom were now on the sex offenders' register. She'd won a car by being the person who could touch it for the longest period of time – four days, 20 hours, 48 minutes and 12 seconds. The other competitor had eventually fallen asleep, slipped and broken his hip. But still, she won a small van.

The stories just kept on coming...

"I bet you've done some crazy things too," she said after about four hours.

I had a little think. Then I kept thinking. There must be something from the world of junior ballroom dancing; a hotbed of intrigue and interest. But nothing immediately sprang to mind.

Before I'd quite finished thinking, Rita was off again.

"I can see we're kindred spirits Scott, we're just mad aren't we? We should hang out, as the kids say these days."

So we (kind of) started going out with each other. Kind of. I gave her a Project Number and got to work – my sole aim being to stop her saying "I'm mad me!" as it is the universal truth that people claiming to be mad are not – they're just annoying.

She'd ring me up at 3 o clock in the morning, "Scott, are you awake?"

"Not really..."

"I couldn't sleep so I got up and started to make a model of the Taj Mahal with matchsticks but I've run out of matchsticks. Could you bring some round?"

"I don't have any."

"There's a twenty-four-hour garage near you isn't there?"

It was fairly near her as well I seemed to recall. "How many do you want?" I asked, wiping the sleep from my eyes.

"About eighteen thousand."

She'd sign us up for anything, particularly charitable endeavours; a 24-hour aerobics class in aid of Save the Children; a 50 mile bike ride in aid of the local library; a parachute jump in aid of the Guide Dogs for the Blind.

She'd apply to go on as many TV quiz shows as she could (someone has to). I'd have to go with her. We got accepted on to some obscure game show on a digital TV channel that I'd never heard of where you had to take an item of clothing off for every question you got wrong.

When I was asked which country is the world's biggest producer of walnuts, I guessed Canada and had to show my walnuts because the answer was China.

"I thought you would have known that, being your native land," said the question master.

"I'm not actually Chinese," I said as I slid my pants off.

Rita was long since naked, having given joke answers to every question fired her way. "Barbara Streisand" was her favourite answer in the Geography round.

In the end I don't think the show was ever broadcast, something to do with allegations of exploitation. Rita was very disappointed.

Even our sex life was bizarre. She wanted everything; role-play, exhibitionism, fetishism, sado-masochism.

"Just bite this…don't worry, it's clean, I promise."

I tried everything I could think of to tone her down; to make her less annoying. I tried to get her interested in the news by glancing at a paper or watching a topical documentary. But that was too dull. I encouraged her to pursue mindfulness and tranquillity but she couldn't stick it. I told her about Ellie-May the Elective Mute and the benefits that had brought her but Rita just thought that was stupid. I tried to guide our conversation towards politics, the arts and the economy but she got bored very quickly and would try to show me how she could make the sound of a fart from her armpit.

When we nearly got arrested for the third time, I was tempted to call it quits. I was incapable of helping her. In the end, she saved me the trouble when she met a parcel delivery man called Jeremy who was "in a band." Rita was seduced by the rock and roll lifestyle that Jeremy promised her. As it turns out, Jeremy played the accordion in a ceilidh folk trio but still…those village halls could get pretty raucous.

Project #1 – Sally Paxton (not alive)

I'll never forget those first few moments upon arriving at school the morning after Sally Paxton had killed herself. The playground was abuzz. Rumour spread like wildfire. People were crying; holding their heads in disbelief. Some just couldn't stop saying, "I can't believe she's dead." Others attempted Gallows' Humour but it was too soon and the comedians quickly lost their nerve.

I could tell the situation was serious because Dave was serious.

"Have you told anyone?" I asked him.

"Told anyone what?"

"About the letter?" I asked feverishly.

"What letter?"

"The letter that I gave you last night. The letter in which I dumped Sally Paxton."

Some other kids turned to have a look at me as I raised my voice; a rare sight. A rare noise from my smiling face.

"Oh, that one. What about it?"

I actually grabbed Dave, by the shoulder straps of his rucksack.

"Don't you see? Yesterday Sally Paxton was alive and well and she had a boyfriend called Second Hand Scott. Today she's dead and she has no boyfriend called Second Hand Scott. Can't you see it? She's dead because of me. She killed herself because of my letter. I killed her."

And I knew it must be true because Dave didn't even attempt to derail me or persuade me otherwise. He just scuffed his shoe into the playground and refused to meet my gaze.

The Head teacher of our school, a Mrs Carmichael, was looking sombre as we all traipsed into the school assembly hall. The entire school body seemed to move in silence, sensing the occasion.

Mrs Carmichael spoke with seemingly genuine remorse to a silent, truly silent, room.

"It is with great sadness that I have to inform you that one of our students, Sally Paxton, died yesterday."

If possible, the room went even quieter. My heart was beating like never before.

"It's not the time or the place to go into details. Those will surely be made known in due course. Perhaps after Christmas. However, I just want to publicly express the condolences of the entire school to the family of Sally Paxton. She was a popular student; clever, bright and enthusiastic and she will be sorely missed."

Project #15 – Wendy the Worst (tenacious)

"The only consistent part of someone's character is their inconsistency."

Wendy didn't respond so I said it again.

"I said, the only consistent part of someone's character is their inconsistency."

Wendy continued looking at her phone.

I had to say it one more time, this time with a fair degree of theatricality, before Wendy acknowledged my presence.

"What the hell are you blathering on about Scott?"

"I was just saying..."

"I know what you were just saying, I've heard you say it a hundred times. What does it mean?"

"It means that sometimes people do things completely out of character for no apparent reason."

Wendy continued to look at her phone.

"And your point is?" she said after allowing me to wait an appropriate length of time.

"The point is then...I suppose...well...the point is this..."

And that was where it got difficult. It was easy at home as I prepared the words. It was easy on the street as I rehearsed the necessary regretful inflections. It was easy as I sat and sipped a coffee, waiting for Wendy to arrive. But all that ease just slipped away when confronted with Wendy herself.

In fact, it wasn't the prospect of Wendy herself that made things hard. It was Sally Paxton. Whenever I thought about upsetting a girl, a vision of Sally Paxton went through my mind. Sally Paxton lying on her bed; a large pill container in one hand and my letter in the other. And that made me say yes, to anything.

The visions of Sally P were swiftly followed by visions of my mum, although those visions were less defined and I wasn't entirely certain why they were there at all. I couldn't think of any way I had hurt my mum beyond the usual childhood laziness and selfishness. I couldn't think of anything I could have done to help her, she was so self-contained.

So even though it was abundantly clear that Wendy had lost interest in me, and even though it was abundantly clear that Wendy was a cow beyond any sort of rehabilitation, the actual act of trying to break up with her was immeasurably difficult.

"The point is this…that I think our relationship might need to, just possibly, come to an end."

There. Said it.

Wendy put down her phone and gave me one of her stares.

"Are you breaking up with me?"

"Well, yes and no, but mainly yes. I suppose."

"Is it because I text other men?"

"No."

"Is it because I pursue other men?"

"No."

"Is it because I fondle other men?"

"No."

"Is it because I'm mean to you?"

"No."

"Is it because I'm mean to other people?"

"No."

"Is it because I use you?"

"No."

"Is it because of the things I make you do in the bedroom?"

"No."

"Is it because of Fleur?"

"What do you mean?" I asked uncertainly.

"You know I have a deep physical attraction for Fleur, albeit unreciprocated. Is it that?"

"No, not that."

Wendy threw her hands up in the air.

"Well Scott, I am at a loss. If it isn't any of that, why are you breaking up with me?"

"I don't know. I just am."

Wendy started to howl, which was a bit uncomfortable bearing in mind the coffee shop was fairly busy. It was obviously fake, but tremendously effective. The tears were patently manufactured. The reddening of her cheeks was contrived. The sobs catching in her throat were clearly well-rehearsed. But still, my heart started to beat, my palms started to sweat – only my smile didn't slip.

"How can you sit there and just smile at me?" she said between sobs. "When you have just broken my heart? Is this why they call you Second Hand Scott, because you have no first hand emotion? You don't feel anything?"

She placed such an emotional emphasis on the word "feel" that the whole shop turned to openly stare. And I imagine they saw what Wendy wanted them to see; a distraught girl sitting opposite a heartless cad and bounder, grinning like a Cheshire cat. (As opposed to a newt, with the rictus of fear on its face, trying to escape the clutches of a ravenous pike).

I'm afraid to say, when she fell to her knees and clasped her hands together, as if praying for mercy before me, that she broke me like a twig.

"Perhaps we could give it another try," I said weakly.

In an instant her fake tears dried up and she resumed her seat.

"Good idea, stay with me until after Christmas at least. I'd like a present if nothing else."

She turned to the audience, "Show's over everyone, nothing more to see. He's taken me back."

Chapter 14

"Jilted"

<u>Project #14 – Joan the Jilted (very successful)</u>

"Scott, you really are a wonderful person."

This was (and is) true. But I made an "oh-shut-up-you-with-your-outrageous-compliments" sort of gesture with my hands and shoulders.

"When I first met you I was a wreck. I was at the very bottom. Broken."

Again, this was true. But I made an "oh-don't-be-so-hard-on-yourself-you-daft-little-thing-you" sort of gesture – this time by scrunching up my face.

When I first met Joan she was in the middle of quite a messy divorce. Messy in a considering-suicide-burning-wedding-photographs-and-bulk-buying-Hobnobs kind of way. Joan's husband – a lazy, computer game obsessed weakling called Terry – had left her for a man. A man! *That man*, as Joan called him. *That poofter*, she said in moments of uncontrolled, politically incorrect rage – of which there were many. Joan had spent most of her marriage to Terry in the firm belief that she was "the catch." She was the kissed, not the kisser. She was certainly the better looking of the two. A man in a bar had once asked Joan if she had ever considered modelling (part-time), as he patted her on the bum. No-one had ever complimented Terry in that way. Terry was so thin and weedy and nerdy that many people assumed he was in remission. When Terry wore a hat, people generally suspected he might be an undernourished refugee. To be jilted by a man that Joan (not so) secretly considered to be beneath her was quite a knock to her confidence. She didn't take it well. In the dislocated months that followed the unilateral split, Joan put on a stone in weight (mainly over the womb) and (re)developed acne, a condition that had afflicted her in her teenage years.

It was this spotty, flabby, homophobic version of Joan that I first encountered in the café at the gym, sobbing discreetly into her post-workout cappuccino. (Although, having spent some time watching her as she traipsed around the gym in a pathetic attempt at exercise, I didn't think she quite justified the generous chocolate sprinkling on her coffee).

"I don't think it's any exaggeration to say that you saved me," Joan said.

No, it wasn't really. But I made an "oh-it-is-an-exaggeration-and-we-both-know-it-you-silly-sausage" kind of gesture with my eyebrows.

"I owe so much to you. You've restored me. You've rebuilt me. My confidence is back, my self-esteem has grown. I feel like I'm truly me again."

Again, I could not disagree. Where once sat a sad and desperate creature with greasy spots, flat hair and a paunchy middle, now sat a woman who had rediscovered her worth. Sleek black hair with a hint of volume, long painted nails, decent posture, a ready smile. This was the Joan I had seen in photographs at her flat; the few that had escaped her pyro maniacal rage. Pictures of fancy dress parties and beach holidays and social occasions. Photographs full of expression: smiles, funny faces and the occasional pout. This was the Joan I knew must be in there somewhere – in amongst the tears and the self-recrimination and the deep hatred of the forty-six-year-old homosexual local radio presenter called Benjamin who had stolen her husband.

"You have put up with so much."

Tears, anger, resentment, late night phone calls to her

husband's answer phone, lonely regret, raging against God, drunken trips to gay bars on the off-chance of seeing Terry, an ill-advised fake tan, building and then burning an effigy of Benjamin the gay DJ, an embarrassing attempt at flirting with the office lesbian...it had been an interesting few months. But I had endured it with aplomb.

Joan started to make a pretence at sobbing. She took a clean tissue out of her new handbag and dabbed gently at her eyes. Her eyes weren't actually wet; such an act of perspiration would play havoc with her expensive and perfectly applied mascara, but she dabbed anyway...as if to convince both of us that she was genuinely upset.

"I owe you so much. Really I do. And that's why I feel so guilty about what I am about to say."

Project #1 – Sally Paxton (deceased)

Christmas Day was one of the worst days of the year in my family home. It was one of only two days a year when my father tore himself away from the high octane world of deep fat frying and spent the day with his family...namely, me and my mum. It was miserable. My father actually had very little to say that wasn't fish or chip related. And my mum had very little to say to my father at all. I could usually be counted upon to spread a little joy...by reciting a specially written Christmas poem or acting out the Nativity using different variations of the Scottish accent.

"We're looking for a wee baby," said the Glaswegian Magi.

But that first Christmas after Sally Paxton had died was different. I couldn't quite bring myself to be jovial. I spent much of the day staring at our Christmas tree; a green and white artificial tree that had seen better days. My parents spent much of the day staring at me, perhaps hoping that I would become possessed by the spirit of Christmas and perform a medley of Cliff Richard's most popular yuletide hits.

Under the tree there were five presents. This was unusual. Uniquely unusual for the Logan household.

It was our family tradition to put off that exciting moment of opening presents until Christmas afternoon – after we had finished working through a tough old bit of Turkey and some recently unfrozen vegetables. If we couldn't have a nice collection of presents, we could at least have some anticipation as we waited to open them.

I opened the present from my parents: "a wash bag, how kind," I mumbled.

"Sorry about the musty smell, I did try to air it," said my mum.

"It smells fine," I lied, subtly placing it downwind.

My father opened his present from me; a book of motivational quotes from great businessmen of the ages. Henry Ford, the maker of cars, was on the front saying something like: "if I had asked people what they had wanted, they would have said "a faster horse.""

"I thought you could read it behind the counter; dip in and out, glean wisdom. Improve your business practices."

He frowned at me.

For my mum, I had purchased a small set of earrings, each shaped like a love heart. They were small and cheap (although new) and she said she loved them. I believed her.

I also had a present from my Auntie Pam, the Lancastrian spinster; a wildlife "annual" suitable for a six-year-old with the price sticker still on the back.

There was also one more.

"Aren't you going to open that one?" asked my mum, slightly intrigued by this additional present. Logan family Christmases only ever involved four presents and this extra present was titillating to us all. Even my father was interested, judging by the raised eyebrows.

I knew who it was from. She'd given it to me a few weeks before; thrusting it into my hand as she walked past me in the corridor at school without a word. I don't know why I'd put it under the tree. To wallow perhaps. To garner sympathy. To be special. To wonder what Christmas should be like. I was regretting it at that moment though.

"Open it," my mum urged.

I opened it with some considerable reluctance.

"Aw, that's nice," said my mum, trying to sound enthused at the sight of a very cheap snow globe.

Project #15 – Wendy / Fleur (decisions)

Fleur, as you can imagine, was looking radiant.

Little black dress, high heels, a good, straight spine and tousled dark hair – she looked amazing. Top drawer.

"Who is that? I'd give her one."

Dave was stroking his nipple through his shirt as he gazed across at Fleur. I nearly punched him as I, once again, bemoaned his appearance at my door that very afternoon.

"Ah, Dave, thanks for coming down, entirely unannounced, but I'm sorry, I've got a works' do…"

"I'll come with you, no worries. I love office parties; chance to chat up some bored little housewife let out for the evening."

"Housewives don't come to office parties…they're housewives," I tried. But he didn't listen and I was compelled to bring him.

Dave had drunk like a fish since arriving at the party; throwing down anything and everything he could get his hands on. The Senior Management Team had placed various drinks around the room and Dave had been in to them all. Or, more to the point, they had been in to him. He had nearly come to blows with Erica, a senior underwriter, over a half-finished bottle of rum. (She could stick it away too).

"And who is this fine specimen of a man?" said Wendy as she appeared at my side, like a different type of spirit.

She was also wearing a little black dress and looked, well quite nice actually. At that precise moment, her face had even temporarily stopped scowling; meaning that Dave was quite taken by the compliment. Truth be told, given his waning good looks and his waxing waistline, he was taken by any compliment.

"They call me Casanova Dave; all-round stud," he said without any degree of self-awareness, self-consciousness or shame.

I wanted to punch him again.

Wendy, on the other hand, seemed quite taken with him too.

"An all-round stud eh? We'll have to see about that...," she said with a wink.

(I hate winkers).

"It's something that has to be seen to be believed..." Dave responded with another wink.

"I've seen a lot of things..." Wink.

I wandered off in search of a drink, leaving Wendy and Dave to wink at each other and trade infantile and witless drivel that they would no doubt classify as "banter."

As I was leaning against the bar, having had to pay for a drink due to Dave's insatiable thirst, I felt the presence of Fleur.

"Scott, you're not smiling..."

In an instant, I was.

"I often wonder how genuine your smile is."

"Do you?"

"Yes. I sometimes..."

Before she could finish her musing and before I could open my heart to her or say something devilishly romantic like, "my smile is only real when I'm with you," Wendy and Dave were at our sides.

"And where is the delectable Leonard this evening?" asked Wendy.

"He's on his way," replied Fleur.

Damn. Hate that guy.

"Not to worry, we have enough slabs of meat here to keep us entertained," Wendy said as she slapped my well-developed pectoral and slid her hand along Dave's well developed gut.

"I'll show you a slab of meat…" started Dave.

I wandered off again, this time in search of the toilet.

A little while later, Dave slumped down heavily next to me.

"Alright Second Hand? You look a bit glum."

"I don't actually have a huge amount to smile about."

"What you talking about?"

"I've got a horrible girlfriend for a start."

"What? Wendy? She's brilliant. I don't think I've met a girl before who can keep up with my banter. She's great."

"If she's so great, please feel free to ask her out."

"I wasn't thinking of asking her out, but I was thinking of having a go on her in the disabled toilet."

"Be my guest."

"Really?"

"Sure."

"You honestly don't mind if I take your girlfriend in the disabled toilet and slip her a length?"

Just at that moment, the music in the room seemed to dim and I heard Wendy's voice float towards me. That snippet of conversation contained the words, "…the problem with disabled people is…"

"Honestly, I don't mind at all," I said.

"Why are you going out with her then if you don't care? You usually try and help these weirdos don't you…not cut them loose for sexual monsters like me?"

"Two words, Sally P."

Dave groaned: "Let it go man, it was nothing."

"Sally Paxton needed me but I couldn't stay the course. I dumped her. I dumped her by letter. And just a few short hours after you delivered that letter, she killed herself. That is not nothing."

I knew Dave didn't disagree with me because he couldn't meet my eye.

"About that letter..." Dave said.

"Yes?"

Dave was working his mouth, as if trying to find the right words. I wished he'd just come out with it and say what he'd been thinking all these years – that yes, I had killed Sally Paxton. That yes, it was my heartless, cold, damning letter that had caused her to ingest as many pills as possible in a short space of time. That yes, I was a killer. A murderer. And I was doomed to my fate...as a romantic accessory...forevermore.

But just as he was clearing his throat, I happened to catch sight of Fleur out of the corner of my eye. She looked upset. Within a second, I was there; reassuring smile to the forefront.

"What's wrong?"

"Leonard's not coming."

Yes!

"Ah, that's a shame," I said. "He'll have to come next year."

"No, he won't be coming next year either. He's just broken up with me. By text."

What a guy!

"By text? Who would do such a heartless thing? I always knew he was no good," I said.

"He said I was too nice."

"That's why girls break up with me," I said, feeling her pain.

"How can someone be too nice?"

"Come here," I said as I placed my nice arms around her nice body and gave her a nice cuddle.

My word, it felt good. The slightest touch of her upper arm during choir practice had been enough for me to fall in love with her. To actually hug her...wow, I fell into an abyss that I knew I would never get out of. (Ridiculous, horribly pretentious statement...but true. At that moment I wanted to run in whimsical fashion through a beautiful and sun-soaked meadow singing at the top of my lungs about the beauty of life whilst stroking butterflies and bestowing kindly smiles on spotless lambs). And when she nuzzled her head into my shoulder I got a glimpse of what heaven must be like.

But unfortunately that tender moment was ruined when Wendy wrenched Fleur's arm from around my waist.

"And what is the meaning of this?" Wendy bellowed.

"Scott was just comforting me," said Fleur.

"My boyfriend comforts no-one without my authorisation."

"He was just being kind."

"And where does kindness stop? Hugs? Kisses? Sweet nothings? Impregnation?"

"You're being ridiculous," said Fleur.

"Am I? I've seen the way he looks at you."

"So have I," added Dave, rather unhelpfully, having joined the gathering throng of curious observers.

"Deny it Scott...if you dare!" Wendy boomed.

I looked at Fleur and Fleur looked at me and I couldn't bring myself to deny it. Once again, I just failed to speak. I raised my eyebrows in a "yep-you-got-me" sort of way.

"You see? Perhaps this innocent hug wasn't as innocent as you might have thought. This is why they call him Second Hand Scott...because he likes a girl in each hand," Wendy re-boomed.

"Is that why they call you Second Hand Scott?" Fleur asked.

"No..."

"It's because he likes sloppy seconds, that's why we call him that," Dave guffawed.

"Shut up Dave."

"Why did you need comforting anyway? I would have done it if I'd known. I've always wanted to comfort you," Wendy said as she threw open her arms with the offer of a hug. Fleur declined.

"Leonard and I have broken up."

"Perfect for you mate, get her on the rebound like all the others!"

"Shut up Dave," I pleaded.

"Are you vulnerable?" asked Wendy of Fleur.

"I'm fine, thank you."

"Scott loves vulnerable girls – it's his speciality. Get in there son."

"Shut up Dave," I shouted.

The whole office party had come to a halt now as everyone gathered round to watch. I tried to remember just how many times this kind of thing had happened to me – being the reluctant centre of attention in a public tangle of romance and recriminations.

"Why do they call you Second Hand Scott?" Fleur asked. "You've never told me."

"It was because we didn't have much money when I was growing up and my mum was spotted..." I started.

"No it's not!" shouted Dave. "It's because he picks up girls that have just been dumped. He gets them when they're vulnerable; that's his speciality. Or he gets the ones that no-one else will take on – ugly, annoying, whatever, he's not fussy."

All eyes turned to Wendy – wondering just what category she fell into.

"Is this true?" asked Fleur. "Is that why you were comforting me?"

"No, it's not like that. Not with you. I promise."

"He calls them his Projects." Dave was really getting into it, finding it hilarious.

"Projects?" Fleur folded her arms under her breasts – a bad sign. "Projects?"

I tried to explain...but couldn't really. Not in a pithy little sentence; it was too complicated. Dave didn't worry...

"Project number 1, Nicola Big Nose. She tried to chat me up in sixth form but I told her to bugger off. Scott had a bash at her outside the Pig and Whistle while she was still crying."

This wasn't sounding good.

"Project number 2 was some bird he picked up in a club. She'd just seen her boyfriend copping off with someone else so she needed a bit of comfort. Scott gave her that alright. He was all over her like a rash. Well out of his league too; he couldn't have got her any other time."

Not sounding good at all.

"Project number 3 was some lesbian who wanted a boyfriend to throw her parents off the scent. Scott was well up for that; a bit of lesbo action. I could go on if you want…"

There was an uneasy silence in the room. I think most people would have liked Dave to carry on with the list but Fleur was looking at me in a new way; a way that I didn't like. And I think I probably deserved it.

"Well, I know one thing for certain, I'm no project," said Wendy.

"Is this true? That you use girls like this?" asked Fleur.

"I don't use them. I let them use me. It's really very different and not quite so much fun. I know it sounds wrong but I was just trying to help. I don't like seeing girls in pain. Never have."

"I am no project!"

"I've told him he's a sexist," said Dave.

"Shut up Dave."

Fleur was looking at me again and that sun soaked meadow seemed to have disappeared forever. The butterflies were shying away from my stroking hand and the spotless lambs were giving me disapproving looks.

"I don't know what to think of you anymore," said Fleur.

"Scott, we're leaving." Wendy beckoned me like an owner beckons a dog. I took a step…

"Is she one of your Projects? Is that why you let her speak to you like that?" asked Fleur. "You hinted as much at the nature reserve."

"Of course I'm not a Project," asserted Wendy. She glared at me, daring me to contradict her. I dared.

"She's Project number 15. She said she needed me."

"Why? Why does that matter?" Fleur asked.

"Sally Paxton," I said.

"Who's Sally Paxton?"

I tried to explain...about her reputation, her issues, her potential, that letter. About how I wanted to help her. About how there was something within me that wanted to help someone, anyone, and that I'd chosen her. And I'd given it my best shot; compliments, empathy, affection – the whole caboodle. But then she'd died – one of the worst possible deaths.

The whole room was listening. The post boy, the receptionist, the underwriters, the senior management team – they all got an anecdote that evening. There was an uneasy silence when I finished my tale of woe but Fleur eventually summed up the mood of the room:

"You're a bit thick aren't you Scott?"

"Yes I am," I agreed. (The senior management team nodded their agreement also).

"I'm sorry about Sally Paxton though," said Fleur. "That must have been hard. But just because a very complicated girl killed herself, it doesn't mean that you have to just assume it was your fault."

"But it was. My letter..."

"About that letter..." interrupted Dave. There was something in his tone of voice that made everyone listen to him. All eyes turned his way. He scuffed his shoe against the floor like some naughty school boy.

"Go on," I said.

"I never gave it to her," he mumbled.

"Sorry?" (I had heard).

"I never gave it to her. The letter."

Bloody hell.

"I forgot."

I edged my way towards him.

"You forgot?"

"Yes."

"You just forgot?"

"Yes."

"So why didn't you tell me earlier? That you had just forgot? Like fifteen years ago."

"I don't know," said Dave as he looked at the floor again.

"You do know. And I think I know too, but tell me anyway."

I was still advancing upon him.

"Alright," said Dave reluctantly. "I didn't just forget. I went round there to give Sally the letter and I...erm...well...I shagged her."

Silence. Silence in that busy, celebratory room. The room had been quiet before; intrigued, interested, curious – the silence of not wanting to miss a vital detail in a convoluted story. But now it was truly silent, just like that assembly hall when Mrs Carmichael announced that Sally Paxton was dead. It was the silence of those with bated breath. The silence of those who knew that something significant had just occurred.

I hadn't killed her after all. Dave had.

"So you probably shouldn't blame yourself that she's dead," Dave said.

Wendy placed an appreciative hand upon Dave's arm, "You are a bad boy aren't you?"

I advanced further.

Dave smiled at Wendy, "well, I wouldn't say that..."

I advanced further.

"You killed her," I said, not a hint of a smile upon my face.

Dave had already become distracted by Wendy's upper thigh, which was being pressed against his. But even she edged away when she saw the look on my face. Leaving Dave all alone.

"You killed her. That sweet girl. You killed her."

Dave looked shocked. "Me? I didn't kill her. She killed herself you numpty."

"Because of you. Because of what you did to her."

"I didn't do anything. We just had a bit of fun and then she gave me a snow globe and told me to bugger off. Tried to read some crap song lyrics to me but I wasn't interested."

"You killed her."

"Don't be such an idiot Second Hand. It's not like China, you know, where you have to stab yourself if you feel a bit sad. This is the real world."

"You killed her."

I was edging forward and Dave, for a wonder, was edging back.

"You're an idiot. She killed herself. She was a lunatic. One minute she's cutting her arms and the next minute she's running away from home. Then she's trying to burn the school down and then she's kicking a teacher. She was a complicated girl. If you think she would kill herself just because I had sex with her you're stupid. Life isn't as straightforward as that."

"You killed her."

He was against a wall now.

"You know I didn't kill her."

"All those years I thought it was me."

"Ha!" Dave laughed. "You never thought it was you, not really. They didn't even mention your stupid letter at the inquest. You just wanted to be someone. You wanted to be a martyr. You wanted an excuse to suck up to all these girls. You wanted an excuse to piss your life away. You remember that night with Sonya Peel? You were jabbering on about Sally

Paxton all night and then as soon as you saw Sonya you were off like a shot, trying to get into her knickers. Don't try to blame me just because you're an idiot. You went out with Sally Paxton because you wanted a girlfriend and she was the only option you had."

"I wanted to help her."

"You wanted to help yourself. That's the truth of it. Get some love somewhere. And I don't blame you. I mean, look at your parents."

That stopped me a little. "What do you mean?"

"Well, we all know what your mum got up to when she was younger and everyone knows your dad makes her suffer for it. But still, she doesn't leave does she? She's still there...with him...in silence...everyday...even though they hate each other. You grew up in that so I don't blame you for anything."

I wound back my fist.

Fleur said something like, "Scott, don't..." but it seemed to come from far away.

I had one of those moments, as I put my little fist up in the air, where things become fairly clear. Elements of my past started slotting into place; facts and circumstances that I had chosen to resolutely and consistently ignore came back to bite me with the vengeance of the overlooked. Aspects of my future started to shape before me; potentialities floated around my head, taunting me.

I thought of Fleur; delicious, pleasant Fleur. And I thought to myself, I could turn round now and kiss that girl in a wonderfully romantic moment and we could walk out of that office party and into the sunset, leaving Dave's face entirely unmarked and my fist completely un-bruised. And I could have a proper relationship with her; one of love and respect and a mutual love of banality and social conscience, peppered with close harmony singing and bird watching. And when I had matured as a person and gained some measure of emotional depth, I could take Fleur home with me to meet my mum and we could all have a good grown up chat about how my mum needn't be sad anymore and that one mistake needn't ruin a life.

Or, I thought to myself, I could turn round now and try to kiss Fleur in a wonderfully romantic fashion and receive a slap for my trouble and for being a misogynistic, sexist pig. And Wendy would laugh and Fleur would be offended and my work colleagues would spend the rest of the evening talking about my folly and exaggerating it with each re-telling and I would be forced to look for another job rather than face the tidal wave of gossip that would flow around me on Monday morning.

Or, I thought to myself, I could turn round now and dump Wendy in spectacularly melodramatic fashion and get some conceited pleasure out of it. I could tell her that my days of being a Project driven individual were over. I could denounce her for being the most unpleasant, unappealing, unlikeable, unredeemable person I had ever met. It might even let me recover a modicum of self-respect amongst my colleagues.

Or, I thought to myself, I could turn round now and Wendy could have left already, bored by my petty concerns – off to seek another sucker to dominate and oppress. And whilst my back was turned, Dave might sneak out after her and they might find themselves in a dark alleyway.

Or, I thought to myself, I could start to deal with the real issue and go home to confront my parents. I could speak up and speak out for the first time in my life and bring some light into their bored, sad little lives. Or I could head home with the best of intentions and my father could just stare at me until I left again and my mum would be sadder than before.

But then I thought, no. *Stop thinking of yourself in relation to the nearest female; whether it be pleasant Fleur, horrible Wendy or your imperfect mum. You're not an accessory. You're not an aspect of someone else. You are Second Hand Scott no longer. You don't have to accept the unacceptable anymore. You don't have to smile through everything – insults, slights, disparagement. You don't have to go with the flow for fear of upsetting someone. You can do whatever you like. You can lead your own life and, let's face it, you've done a pretty bad job of trying to help other people with theirs.*

Something my mum once said floated back to me: "And after you have suffered a little while..." I couldn't quite remember the rest.

So I asked myself, "what is it that you want to do? What do you really want to do? Right at this moment?"

Regardless of the consequences...?

And the answer was...punch Dave.

So I did.

About G.A. Milnthorpe

Gavin Milnthorpe is a commercial lawyer by day, and a writer of fictional nonsense by night. Second Hand Scott is his second novel. He has had some (small) success in writing for the stage. He can also be found trying his hand at stand-up comedy in and around East Anglia which, as his audiences will attest, is no laughing matter. He is married (punching above his weight) and is the father to two small (wonderful) children.

Connect with G.A. Milnthorpe

Twitter: @GavMilnthorpe

Other Book(s) by G.A. Milnthorpe

'Stanley Young is Planning a Murder in a Very Precise and Intricate Manner' (Arena Books) (2013)

Stanley Young has spent years perfecting a carefully constructed murderous plan. Every angle has been considered and every eventuality pondered. One ordinary Friday, Stanley, under the guise of carrying out his normal routine of inspection and interviews, carefully plants the seeds of deception and prepares the necessary tools to carry out his nefarious scheme. But will he have the guts to go through with it?